Black Fox Literary Magazine is a print and online literary magazine published biannually.

Copyright © 2022 by *Black Fox Literary Magazine.*

All Rights Reserved.

Issue 23 Cover Art: *Carpe Librum (Maastricht)* by Gregg Chadwick

ISBN: 978-1-7336240-9-1

Editor's Note

Welcome to Issue 23! Thank you for your patience, we know this is a much-anticipated issue for many of our contributors and readers. We are happy to launch this summer issue into being while it is still, indeed, summer!

Congratulations to our "Fault Lines" contest winner: Theresa Sylvester. Theresa is a Zambian writer currently based in Western Australia. Her excellent work of fiction, "Blank Speech Bubbles" was a unanimous favorite among our readers. Thank you to the many writers who participated in our summer contest.

Inside this issue we are happy to include writers from across the country as well as a few from across *both* ponds. We are proud to continue to feature new voices among the more seasoned writers, and this issue includes multiple BIPOC authors and previous Pushcart nominees. We continue to attract authors and poets working with a wide variety of styles within many genres, who persist in pushing against literary boundaries. We hope our readers enjoy this as much as we do!

As always, we thank all of our contributors, present and past. We are honored to feature your work in our pages.

We are truly yours,

~ The Editors
Racquel and Elizabeth

Meet the BFLM Staff

Editor:

Racquel Henry is a Trinidadian writer, editor, and writing coach with an MFA from Fairleigh Dickinson University. She is also the Editor-in-Chief at *Voyage YA Journal* and owns the writing studio, Writer's Atelier, in Maitland, FL. Racquel has been a featured author, presenter, and moderator at writing conferences and MFA residencies across the US. She is the author of the novelette, *Holiday on Park, Letter to Santa, Christmas in Cardwick*, and *The Writer's Atelier Little Book of Writing Affirmations*. Her fiction, poetry, and nonfiction have appeared in various literary magazines and anthologies. When she's not working, you can find her watching Hallmark Christmas movies.

Managing Editor:

Elizabeth Sheets is a writer and an editorial assistant for the *Journal of Proteome Research*. She earned a MA in Narrative Studies from Arizona State University. As a student, Elizabeth developed a passion for prison education. She has taught writing classes inside local prisons and corresponds with inmate writers about their creative work. Elizabeth enjoys a wide variety of different reading material. Some of her favorite authors are Roxane Gay, Stephen King, Anne Rice, Fredrik Backman, Kristen Arnett, and Sarah Waters. Elizabeth's fiction, nonfiction, and poetry appear in *Kalliope – A Consortium of New Voices, Black Fox Literary Magazine, Mulberry Fork Review,* and *Apeiron Review.*

Social Media Manager:

Megan Fuentes is an author and the administrative assistant for Writer's Atelier. Her favorite things in the world include iced coffee, office supplies, and telling you about those things. And writing, too. And lists! She is @fuentespens online, and her website is https://fuentespens.ink.

Reader:

H. Rae Monk is a writer based in Mesa, Arizona. She was the first graduate from the Narrative Studies MA program at Arizona State University and holds a BA from ASU in English: Creative Writing with a focus on Fiction. Some of her favorite writers are Anthony Horowitz, Joy Harjo, Matt Goldman, Dina Nayeri, Philip Pullman, and J.R.R. Tolkein.

Contents:

Cover Art

Carpe Librum (Maastricht) by Gregg Chadwick

Blank Speech Bubbles
By Theresa Sylvester
Winner of the 2022 *Black Fox* "Fault Lines" Writing Contest

There's always that one ex.

The one who texts you out of nowhere on Friday at 4:11 a.m.: *Hey!* Making you smirk into the dark as you count in your head how long it's been since you broke up.

"Who is it?" A disembodied voice startles you.

Quickly, you press the lock button and put the phone back on the bedside table. Darkness blankets the room again.

"Jane." Your cousin's name slips through your teeth in a whisper, out into the air, answering your drowsy husband's question.

1, 2, 3, 4, 5...He's snoring again. You exhale, relieved. Then the absence of guilt surprises you. Guilt for what? You've done nothing wrong. It's not your fault The Ex decided to initiate contact after five years, and although it's engraved on your mind, his number isn't in your contacts. You slide one foot out of the duvet and your body feels cooler immediately.

*

Congratulations! I hear you're married now. You almost spit your orange juice out, but you compose yourself and put your phone face down on the rattan table and turn your attention back to your husband. He's telling the new neighbours—whose visit interrupted your lazy Sunday afternoon out on the balcony—the story of how you met.

Your version is shorter: you went to the same primary school, bumped into each other at a church-organised high school leavers party, exchanged numbers, he messaged twice but you always left him hanging. Fast forward to the time you attended a job interview and—surprise!—he was on the panel. As the Assistant HR Manager, he called to tell you that, unfortunately, you didn't get the job, but he could make a few phone calls. He got you a job, and in a week's time, you'll be celebrating five months of marriage.

In his version, the word *patience* pops up a lot.

Under the table, he places a hand on your bouncing knee, silently asking you to be present. You get up to refill the nearly empty jug of juice, hoping to be alone for a minute so you can forward the silly message from The Ex to your cousin Jane, and tell her about this couple from the adjoining flat. But the wife follows you, complimenting the matching stainless-steel appliances, the fresh linen scent from the wall-mounted air fresheners, the transparent beads on your fringe braids, your floor sweeping maxi skirt.

You smile politely, knowing you won't be friends with someone so talkative.

*

The third text vibrates against your thigh while you're peering into the fridge and crunching a carrot.

I'm in town till Friday. Would like to see you for a bit.

Your short-sleeved powder-blue shirt is still tucked into your navy skirt, even though you've been home for ten minutes. It's that time of the day before you transition from gainfully employed woman to wife. From the computer to the stove.

Your thumb hovers over the keypad, tempted to reply, but without your sharp confidante, Jane, telling you how to *handle these men*, your response will be bland. She *Haha'd* the last two texts you forwarded her. She really must be enjoying her impromptu holiday down there in South Luangwa, going on safari tours, swimming in those pools with light blue water you saw on the website of the lodge she's staying at with her big shot government minister. Could never be you! Twenty-three years old and you can't look at a belt without getting flashbacks of your mother, explaining with each thrashing that routines were there for a reason. *Kukontolola*, as she used to call it. And control you she did.

Jane likes to joke that you should have been born sisters because you are closer than your (fraternal twin) mothers. Although you agree, there were many times growing up you caught yourself wondering why you were born to the sour-faced, belt-wielding twin, and Jane, who was forever testing how far she could push the line, got the easy-going, hugs-everybody mother.

You close the fridge and lean your back against it. You're craving something outside this flat. It's on the tip of your tongue, teasing your taste buds. A pizza? A chicken shawarma? Surely, your husband wouldn't object to just one night of takeaway, would he? For close to five months, you've stood in front of the stove or hunched over a brazier on the balcony when the power is out and served him nothing but home-cooked meals. But what would your mother say if she found out you fed your husband takeaway? Worse still, that you messaged him to pick it up on his way home?

At a cousin's bridal party, a month after your own, someone who was relocating approached you to pass her capable maid on to you so as not to leave the woman jobless.

"Maid *wachani*? My daughter can manage. I taught her everything," your mother answered on your behalf and nudged you toward the queue to the food table.

So, you manage by waking up before sunrise to sweep, mop, wash, iron.

To some people, there's nothing glamorous about filing and managing a CEO's diary and booking flights even though you've never been on a plane yourself, but you love your job. It's the only area of your life out of your mother's reach. Only because she has never worked in an office, otherwise she'd disregard your diploma in Secretarial and Office Management and insist you do things her way.

The wall clock reads 5:45 p.m. Would your husband turn the car around if you called him now?

Closed mouths don't get fed and good girls don't get spoiled. Trust Jane to remix a good maxim so she can justify her lifestyle. She's right, though. Good girls stay home and cook nshima with fresh kapenta and cabbage for supper.

*

Your silence speaks volumes. I get it. I'll never bother you again.

Now this one makes you turn the ignition off. You reread it. The Ex's voice is so clear and blameless it pierces your heart in that way you had promised yourself to never feel again.

"Everything okay, neighbor?" Other tenants ask before hopping into their cars to leave for work.

You tell them all the same thing, "Everything's fine. Thanks."

Soon, your red Honda Fit is one of several cars left in the car park. The others belong to the housewives and the informally employed like your new neighbors—the wife owns a hair salon.

Your husband left early because he has month end reports to run.

The morning is unfolding brightly around you. The gardener is chatting and laughing with the maid from flat eleven at the gate, while the child she's supposed to be walking to school stands beside her like a little statue. The clock is ticking. Your right knee bounces faster as you wrestle your conscience over what you're about to do.

After getting off the phone with HR, you stress about not having sounded sick enough, and about them finding someone to fill in for you on short notice.

What would Jane say? You don't always take her advice, but it's nice to hear what someone who is so carefree would do.

"Twenty-three is too young to get married," she'd said when you told her you had accepted your husband's proposal. "You haven't even lived! You don't even have regrets."

Your cousin couldn't understand you had to outsmart your mother before she found you a man to marry.

I'm free now. Let's meet somewhere private and talk. You reply to The Ex and throw your phone onto the passenger seat.

His almost instant response makes you gape. *Room 5, Mukwento Guest House in Roma.*

You shake your head. *Too private. Anywhere else?*

I'm not trying to be funny. I'm lodging here. You know Lusaka better than I do. Choose somewhere where you'll be comfortable...Thanks for replying. I'm happy to hear from you.

You press your head into the headrest. Butterflies flutter in your stomach. Your fingertips tingle. Two minutes go by. You avoid looking in the rear-view mirror because sometimes your features blur into your mother's.

Please don't overthink it. Just come. My room is at the back, it's secluded. No one will see you. I promise. We can keep the door open if you want.

He knows you're second-guessing yourself right now. That's how well he knows you.

*

The door with a gold five screwed into it is open at a thirty-degree angle. The patterned gray-and-white vinyl tiles are making you dizzy, and you haven't even entered the room yet. From here you can see the foot of the bed. No one's around. The narrow corridor is empty, but you don't want to risk being seen, so you knock quickly. The Ex appears in the doorway, smiling wide, bare-chested, white towel wrapped around his waist.

"Hi." His voice is still as bassy as you remember.

You fight the smile tugging at the corners of your heavily lip-glossed mouth. "Hi."

"I apologize," he says, sweeping an arm over his body. "Had to take a quick shower. I was texting you from bed."

He steps aside to let you in, and you catch a whiff of mouthwash and herbal soap. The scents take you back to the college days when he lived in that boarding house near campus.

You walk in and sit on a burnt orange padded chair facing the hastily-made double bed he was messaging you from. He's got clothes laid out to wear. You direct your eyes away from the dark blue trunks with a red elastic to the voile curtains. He grabs his things and heads to the bathroom to get dressed, leaving you with the image of his abs.

As promised, he left the front door open. You could leave without saying a word. Walk away before anyone sees your car in the car park hidden behind the building with the word *Reception* painted on the wall in black. But you sit there, listening to him moving in the next room, recalling things you wish you had forgotten. The dark, lightning bolt shaped birthmark on his right thigh. The coin-sized scar on his left butt cheek he said was from the misadventures of his childhood in Solwezi.

Why am I even here?

Before you answer your question, the bathroom door opens. The Ex comes out wearing a white long-sleeved linen shirt over gray chino shorts. He sits on the bed facing you.

"How are you?" he asks.

"Fine."

"Thanks for coming."

You tighten your grip on the straps of your handbag, cradled in your lap. There are voices out in the corridor, two cleaning ladies giving each other a quick rundown of rooms that can be cleaned now and which ones (like number five) will advise when ready.

"What's in the bag?" He asks.

"You wanted to see me so we can discuss the contents of my handbag?"

He laughs, shaking his head. "Just trying to break the ice."

"You wanted to see me." You repeat this to emphasize this meeting wasn't your idea. "Here I am."

His smile falters. "What time do you have to be at work?"

"I'll go as soon as we're done," you say, looking at your wristwatch.

The look of helplessness shadows his bearded face. He rolls his sleeves. Neither of you knows what to do with this awkwardness. Five years is too long. And before that, the agonizing month leading to your breakup.

"This is hard," he says, rubbing the back of his neck.

Hearing him admit he is struggling to put his feelings into words brings tears to your eyes. You lower your gaze to his bare feet, but it only makes things worse because there was a time when these big feet touched yours under the covers. The tears drip before your hands reach your face and when The Ex asks, "Can I hold you?" your resolve weakens, and your voice pours out of you, tasting like shards of bottled-up pain.

*

When his teeth graze your neck, you're not thinking about the earnestness with which your husband said his wedding vows or what your mother would do if she found out.

*

You're thinking about how clever it is that your hands remember where exactly to touch the man in front of you. How good it feels to hear gasps escape his lips. How he tastes familiar and yet different at the same time.

*

The door is closed.

The Ex locked it and the rest of the world out when clothes started flying off. The uneasiness from before has disappeared. The universe has shrunk and folded into this bed where you're laying side by side under a crumpled white sheet, bringing each other up to speed on people you went to college with. Who is still with who? Who had kids with who? Who died? Who went to prison? Laughter, slow kisses, and quiet hugs interrupt the words coming out of your mouths.

The Ex asks after your parents, whom he never met for the entire duration of your year-long relationship because, even though you were eighteen, your mother forbade you to date. When you tell him your mother is still running a restaurant in Thornpark market, you see a short, tireless woman with long gray plaits hidden under a mesh hair net. And your father: a slim, spiritless man still working at that dry cleaners in town. The Ex met Jane twice when she came home on holiday from Namibia, where she was studying for a Bachelor of Arts in Advertising. In the letters you wrote to each other, she said it amazed her how people keep relationships secret. Now, she's having an affair with a married politician who demands absolute secrecy.

A pang of jealousy shoots through you when The Ex shows you picture after picture of a nice, four-bedroomed house, sitting on a two-acre property, but you say "Wow!" and "Beautiful!" And pretend you aren't curious about the woman in the background of some shots.

His job in the mines pays well, but he took time off to travel to Lusaka because he and the man who owns this guesthouse are looking at going into the accommodation business together. You're proud of the man The Ex has become. He seems so accomplished. So focused.

*

As expected of old lovers, the past creeps into conversation and you reminisce.

The first thing he noticed about you is that you were always alone and you wore ridiculously long skirts. He was in his second and final year of getting his diploma in Public Relations so he knew you were new because he hadn't seen you around campus before. You didn't know that at lunch, while you were sitting under a tree, blowing on those hot, oily but delicious chips in the brown paper bags from the outside kiosks, someone had been watching you for two weeks. Instead of hanging out with his friends at the hostels,

The Ex started sitting under nearby trees just so you'd notice him and not get alarmed when he worked up the courage to talk to you.

One day, he waved. And you hesitantly waved back. He asked if he could join you because the maintenance guys had trimmed his tree and the sun was frying him. You nodded, carried on reading your shorthand handouts. Unless prompted, you were mute. The next day, he gave you a picture of a timid looking male cartoon character sitting under a tree next to a voluptuous female. Between them were two speech bubbles. In the male's cloudy bubble, he had handwritten: *Will you be my friend?* He swears you stared at the picture for close to three minutes before scribbling your reply: *My hips aren't that big.* He laughed and then you laughed.

You love hearing him tell this story. When he pulls the sheet off your body to verify the size of your hips, you playfully hit him with a pillow.

*

It's 1 p.m. Your lunch hour, but neither of you want for anything. You stay glued to the bed, to each other. Until you remember that sometimes, your husband likes to check in with you over the office landline, and you scramble out of the bed to get your phone from your bag.

Startled, The Ex sits up. "What's wrong?"

"I need to call my husband," you say, checking for missed calls and messages from him. There aren't any, but you dash into the bathroom and lock the door behind you.

Your husband picks up on the second ring, apologizing for being quiet today. He's swamped, he explains. You rearrange the toiletries on the sink, say you understand, then mention in passing that the phones in the office are malfunctioning today so he should call you on your phone if need be. Otherwise, just text. When the call ends, you pee, freshen up a bit, gurgle some mouthwash, all without looking at yourself in the wide wall mirror.

*

The Ex is still in bed, arms folded behind his head, staring at the ceiling. He maintains this stiff position even after you snuggle up next to him.

"What's your husband like?" he asks after a while.

You freeze. Sensing your apprehension, The Ex untangles himself from your arms and rolls over to face you. "Relax, I don't mean in bed. If he was great, you wouldn't be here."

An embarrassing warmth covers your naked body. "I didn't come here for sex."

When he notices you closing your legs, he laughs. "Relax, I'm just joking."

You want him to stop saying *relax*.

He places a warm hand on your belly. "Come on, I'm just messing around."

"Is that why you asked me to come? For sex?" You hate yourself for asking. For the hurt in your voice.

"Let's change the subject. You're getting worked up." He gives your belly a quick rub, gets up, and opens the bar fridge. "Damn. Only one bottle of water left," he says, unscrewing the lid. The plastic crackles and shrinks as he gulps down the liquid.

To prove that you're not getting worked up, that you can be an adult about this, you soften your voice and ask, "What's your girlfriend like? I glimpsed her in the photos you showed me."

You expect him to deny it, to say, "You mean my cousin" or "My friend," but he cocks his head to the side and swishes the last of the water from cheek to cheek as though thinking.

"She's fun," he says.

"How so?"

"She has a personality like your cousin Jane. Never a dull moment. For my last birthday, we did the double bungee in Livingstone and for hers, we went to Cape Town for the Dune Thrasher experience. Even at work, she has the same attitude. She's just one of those people who go for what they want, you know?"

You're not sure what's worse. The fact that the woman he is describing is the polar opposite of you or that he compared her to Jane, whom he said was too wild for his liking after their initial meeting. It had pleased you hearing him say that about your cousin because even though you raved about her all the time, you were afraid he'd see her shapely legs and cleavage and wish he had met her first. Your mother didn't allow tight clothing or anything that exposed your chest or legs. Throughout your school years, you always wore thick tights underneath what one popular girl described as your "overly modest" uniforms.

When the time came to buy clothes for college, your mother accompanied you to Mandevu Market and bought you every maxi skirt and dress in sight.

Oblivious to the storm brewing within you, The Ex joins you on the bed again and holds up a plastic laminated menu for you to browse together. You stand up, fling the duvet to the floor. "If your girlfriend is so great—"

"What are you doing?" The Ex cuts you off.

"I'm looking for my underwear!"

He puts his hand under his pillow, pulls out the lacy, maroon underwear but doesn't hand it over. "You and me...We went through something terrible but there were good times as well—"

"Why would you even bring it up?" You reach over to snatch your underwear, but he's too quick.

"The abor—"

You thump your fists into the mattress before he can finish the word. "Stop!"

You cover your ears with your hands, blocking out that awful word, the memory. But it's too late. You're hurtled back to the boarding house, half naked on his bed, sweating and gnashing your teeth.

The metal was cold. Rough. Invasive. You prayed the Clinical Officer knew what he was doing because all that prodding and shoving down there didn't feel right. He told The Ex that he had been sceptical about doing the procedure in a student's room because silence is imperative to avoid attracting attention. "But *gelo waako niwokosa.*"

You lay there, silent tears spilled into your hair as this stranger said that unlike the other female students he'd assisted before, you were strong. You wished The Ex could look at you or hold your fisted hand, but he stood there, staring at the ugly, sagging floral curtains blocking out the light.

*

You were careful.

Even your first kiss was with a boy who lived far away from your neighborhood.

It was your first school holiday away from home. Your mother had finally agreed to let her sister have you for three weeks. "Asisi, she's fourteen and has never spent a night away from home. Let her come and spend some time with her cousin."

You watched your mother's knee bounce up and down, knowing the answer was a no.

"*Muleke ayende mwana*," your father's voice came from behind the newspaper hiding his face. Let the child go. You were so happy you hugged him. As you climbed into the backseat of your Aunty's RAV4, you tried to remember when your father had ever spoken up for you like that. Nothing sprang forth.

Holidaying at Jane's house was better than visiting. You watched TV late into the night, passed time at Avondale shopping complex and went swimming at the house across the road. While the older brother was inside the house with Jane, the younger one was teaching you how to swim. You were careful though. You wore a T-shirt and leggings into the pool and stopped kissing when his breathing got too heavy.

Over the years, there were other boys, but they were few and far between.

Then you met The Ex. The fear of running into your mother or anyone who might report back to her confined your relationship to his room. You sneaked into his room. He never walked you to the bus stop. On campus grounds you acknowledged each other but mostly stuck to your own set of friends. Sometimes you missed class and spent the entire day in that room.

At home, nothing changed. You never missed your 6 p.m. curfew. You did your assignments after supper, woke up in the middle of the night to study, and brought home impressive results.

You were so careful.

*

The events following that day tumble out as if someone had stuffed them in a heavy suitcase inside a rickety closet.

Exams were around the corner. The year was ending. The Ex had an uncle he could stay with for a few months before heading back home to Solwezi. Or he could try to get a job, anything to keep him in Lusaka so you'd be in the same province. But he might as well have been talking to the wall because although you were in the same room, you weren't there. Instead of going to class or to the library or to a study group, you went to his room, took the Doxycycline and Brufen tablets the Clinical Officer had left you, and curled up in The Ex's bed, only getting up to change the cotton wool wedged between your legs or to go home. You wouldn't look at him or speak to him.

"I didn't know what to do. I didn't know what was going on in your head," he says now, tossing your underwear over.

Someone is walking along the corridor. Their high heels are loud and sharp against the concrete floor. A door opens and shuts, leaving behind a deafening silence.

The Ex gets up and starts getting dressed as well. His eyes keep darting to your flat belly, giving you a dull ache in your groin.

"You didn't have many friends. Your cousin was in another country. We had exams to prepare for—"

"You left me," you say, clasping your bra at the front. "You are a user... a coward."

"You wouldn't let me take you to a private hospital. It was always 'what if my mother?' I did my best. I tried! What was I going to stay in Lusaka for, anyway? How was it going to work after graduation? How were you ever going to leave the house?"

You unsteadily slide your feet into your kitten heels, snatch up your handbag and keys and march to the door, but The Ex jumps in front of you, blocking the way.

"I wanted to keep it, remember?" He looks desperate.

"Let me go," you say.

"Not until you tell me why you came."

A heaviness swells in your chest as the truth you didn't want to admit to yourself barges in: it felt good knowing he still wanted you even though you were shameful. But this is all pointless. Nothing can erase the past. It's a permanent smudge you've covered up so well until today. You shouldn't be here.

"Let me go." Your voice is stern. You've never used that tone with him.

He steps aside, shocked.

You feel him watching you walk down the corridor until you disappear around the corner.

*

Bright light flashes across the room, hurting your eyes.

"I'm sorry, I didn't know you were asleep," your husband whispers and turns the light off. "Are you alright?"

You sit up, slowly, dazed. "What's the time?"

"Half-past six. Are you sick?" He throws his jacket on his side of the bed, comes over to place a cool hand on your forehead.

The afternoon flicks through your mind. Walking away from The Ex. Driving home. Sitting in the tub until the water got cold. Crawling into bed.

Luckily, the bedroom is dim because you don't have a lie ready to explain your swollen eyes, or why you're in bed at this hour, or why there isn't the smell of supper coming from the kitchen.

"I'm so tired... And thirsty." You remember you haven't drunk all day.

Your husband rushes off to the kitchen and brings back a fat tumbler of water. "This is all the cold water we have in this house."

You gasp. You forgot to boil drinking water. "Let's share it," you say, knowing how much he hates warm drinks.

He insists you have it all and sits down next to you, rubbing your thigh through your peach satin night slip. "Long day?"

You nod.

He takes the empty glass from you.

"I know you take pride in the way you run things in the kitchen, but do you want me to get us some takeaway?"

You put your arms around his neck and he envelopes you in a tight hug. There's a hint of sweat mixed with his spicy cologne.

When you tell him what you want to eat, he kisses you on the cheek and leaves to go get it, still in his office shirt and trousers. You lie down, watching the encroaching night shadows, and think of your wedding day.

As she fluffed your veil, your mother whispered into your ear, "*Nasebenza*. My job is done."

You wanted to tell her she had failed. That you had bled for two weeks under her watchful eye, and Jane, whom your mother was certain would come back from university with a baby, not a degree, returned to her mother, unscathed, with stories for days and photo albums bulging with memories. And somewhere in those albums were pictures of you and The Ex embracing in a tiny room. You enclosed them in your letters partly to show off your boyfriend and partly out of fear your mother would find them.

Towards the end of the wedding, when you were shaking hands with guests and thanking them for coming, Jane hugged you and fixed your tiara. She had accepted her bridesmaid role, forgiven you for letting your mother choose another cousin as your maid of honor.

"Maybe you chose well after all." You followed your cousin's eyes. She was looking at your husband, half kneeling beside your mother's seat. They were laughing. "This guy is more your class. He'll forever be running after you. I can see it. It's a good thing you dumped the Solwezi guy." She didn't know what had happened, and you left her to believe she knew you inside out.

Because The Ex had spoken highly of his girlfriend, you feel compelled to defend your husband's honor. You want to tell him your husband has loved you since you were in primary school, but he didn't panic every time you looked past him because he knew you'd end up together some day. He taught you to drive, bought you a car instead of taking you on honeymoon, knows when to leave you alone and when to hold on tight. He says being married to you is like solving a puzzle, but he's a patient man.

You reach for your phone. *He's the type of man to give me the last bottle of water.*

The Ex replies. *Who??? Is this text meant for me?*
You asked earlier what my husband is like.
No reply.

Selected Poems by Tyra Douyon

Family Reunion Special

I am born in a house made of mumbles,
coarse swing-low hums paint the walls,

sloshed water for birds and bread
litter the floors, ashed hands holding the beat

clap with the melody instead.
Our maniacal laughter is strung up

outside on the clothesline for everyone to see,
your silk bras that are too big for my chest,

your panic that is too big to hold in my arms.
I tightrope walk that line with you daily,

pinch my toes around the clothespins
so I won't fall off. I am not ashamed

when you keep toppling over, hold a twisted ankle,
use two thumbs to smile your stubborn mouth.

You are 90 years caged with violence.
With bones echoing against the side of the house.

Your delusions soliloquy's of
the loneliness you let us all taste.

Raised to nurture your own

herd of taking care, you lay your back flat like a bridge,

feed the voice charred pieces of hip, pelvis,
and teeth you pry out with a rusty spoon.

We learn how to stir silent pots and
walk fingers across the other's knee.

Ode to the Sous Chef or How Caribbean Kitchens Sing the Blues

The cloudless blue rim holds the whites in your eyes as you run your
middle finger through the hot oil bouncing off the frying pan. You
peel back the ripe plantain and place
it in your palm then gash the knife through the faded yellow
softness, leaving slices of intent down your wrist like discipline
tallies. The cool breeze wafting in from the screen door blows your
house dress into a tent. Your spine and forearms splinter into curved
rods and sketch home from your skin. We play a game of connecting
liver spots and freckles, deciding which

ones are reminders of shuffling feet and hollow hands, a praise and
worship for good days, and those that bring sour memories of a life
not yet forgotten. You remind me to clean the chicken sitting
crossed-legged in the sink and I pour white vinegar over its body.
We always bathe it before consumption, draining blood and soaking
clotted slime into a second bowl
of swimming bacteria. I reiterate that we are not supposed to rinse
the rind. They say it does nothing but leave a suspect trail of disease
all around the kitchen infecting

everything we touch, but you tell me that's what our people do, have
always done.

Taking heed the cooking skills of white people is a laughable offense. A gruff grunt accompanies an annoyed brush of loose hand and staccato brows, you say plainly,
stay off their internet and help me peel these onions. I say they are taking revenge
on her face and she blinks back the fault lines making puddles in the craters
above her cheeks. She kisses her teeth and pushes her chest out, says

let them try with a little too much bass to pass as indifference. This daily feast sits next to synchronized symphony. Our movements a study of people who keep time with the almost chop of fingers mistaken for meat, the knick of the peeler thought to be skin, the fragrant crush of the pilon, which I always thought looked like a little baseball bat, and its fixture as kitchen centerpiece. This is the place where reality is firmly grasped in your hands. A mistake here can cost, so you instinctively abide by these unspoken rules and drown out any voice

smashing windows and side-stepping barricades to barge in. In your world of patted shadow scalps, of two-step with no partner, of cries with no sound—we stand still in this time, holding on with the dull tips of our knives. I wooden spoon carve this picture in full using all the box colors. The limited-edition deep brown takes your shape and you recognize yourself without using my silhouette as a reminder. It is enough for you to simply be,

away from the thoughts that threaten any semblance of normalcy. I am grateful for this hush, this pin-pricked silence, this echo of breath we share before the stovetop altar. It is our only raised glass, a distraction from what we know comes eagerly in the night when they call.

Where do you go when they take you? Do you need me to pack you soupy leftovers masquerading in butter containers? Sew the trailing hem from the blue Danish cookie tin?

Coloring Book

You stack
  your bones
    into a leaning white tower.

You've learned to leave
  no ragged edges.

A clean plate
  forced to swallow.

What is nourishment to a body
that does not want to be fed?

I call your name in crumbles. You perform
an encore without an audience.

I call my mother with palms full of good noise.
With rainbow bullets loaded in a peds dispenser, say—

Grandma is repeating her order to the waitress.
Grandma is throwing tongue at the taxi driver who teefed her.
Grandma is slow clapping in the living room.
Grandma is teaching Bible stories to her knees.

Grandma is crying so God will not forget to hear.

I'm told—
pour blue paint onto the rug
pirate ship the mattress,
use your arms as sails,
but I hold prison
between my fingers instead

and aim red
for the leaking balloon in your gut,
    The nights filled with your
        full-mouthed weeping.
    My braided smile stuck between two
      slapped hands and plugged ears.
           Orange
      mango-colored dress with stiff sleeves.
    Budding violence in a chamber
   of your own making.
    Grandma says, *why don't you join my chorus?*
   A tone-deaf singer is just another
  unwanted protester muddying the movement.
 But you carry the bridge on your back
anyway.

       Yellow
when you stayed. When you rubbed the chicken legs with lemons so
we wouldn't grow gills. When you walked to the top of the hill and
laid in the sun till nightfall. When you wore thick gold hoops, sang
the stars a prayer with your eyes closed. When you vased the weeds
you grew as flowers.

Green

for the wanting. You're gone now but I hope
you'll stay for just a little longer.
The stoop is yours for the hour.
What's to come will kill us.
Between punches to your throat,
you taught me how to close my eyes,
let them take what they want.

Your wholeness no matter the cost.
The regret in these clenched back hugs.

Selected Poems by Mark Blackford

Day 713

I see the light, turning into the driveway. Still on though it's well
past bedtime. There's a shuffling of clutter coming from her room as
I step back into a fatherhood production perpetually under
construction. I walk in: she's making her bed like an unfunny prop
comic setting their stage. She throws herself back onto her pillow,
pulls covers first to her chest & next a book to her face, upside-
down. Pretends I saw nothing. Tells me *Mom said I could stay up to
read.* She knows
I know she's lying, but if it makes her feel better it's a lie I let her
tell. I fix her covers, tuck her in like a parent should, dog-ear her
book so, tomorrow, she can pick up her lie right where she left off
the night before. I lean in to give her a hug and kiss, & hold on long
enough for her to huff my collar, judge my breath and make her own
assessment, before laying her head back down to sleep knowing that
tonight she is wrong. I flick out the light and take my leave,
counting more steps along a long, long way to go.

Sisyphean

The breeze reeks of rain and again
you pour gas into the mower, thinking

you may not have enough to get it done.
You pause, remark at how Nature's breath

stinks like bad things to come and
you want to run inside, write it down

in your notebook: Another poem about
alcoholism. This fix-it list is loaded

with so much you've broken, so
you grab the throttle, pull the cord,

start counting your steps. Like sobriety,
you've put this off for way too long.

You think of your daughter, convinced

all the world's stinging insects are
waiting in this tall grass, to kill her.

For weeks she's been afraid to play outside.
Even more-so, to ask you to do something about it.

Selfishness & neglect bring us all together
today. The lawn's giving you nothing but

grass caking up around blades. The mower
clunks, rattles, sputters, & dies.

After each stall you curse and a head appears,
peers out the window, like Persephone

supervising Sisyphus, this Briggs & Stratton
the boulder you've made yourself to push.

Your dog, confused, has taken to
shitting wherever she sees fit.

The smell rises as you mulch through
it, binds to the hair inside your nostrils

& still you push on, no matter that
it will all soon grow back. When

she hears the *clack* of the throttle bar falling
forward, she'll burst out the front door,

safe and happy. You won't have time to tell her
about the mulched-up shit strewn about the grass

and what would it matter? In this moment,
neither of you can be sure exactly

what you're stepping into
        but it's soft.

One last bash in Nebraska
By Cat Dixon

I wore a tight pink floral dress to the party. I sashayed through every
room. White blooms on my hips and breasts attracted the host who
followed me upstairs to the nectar, and downstairs to the back door.
He drooled like those who came before. Bored and sloppy drunk, I
captured another, but he was colorblind and rude or an imbecile, and
excused himself from the room to chase down a rotting cornhusk.
The fictional welt on my neck, a bursting web I had spun, labeled
me criminal—shunned and caged. With the *O* stuck in their throats,
with compassion out of reach, neither man offered me a glass of
water, neither reached for my hand at night's end, neither had teeth.
I slept in my dress in the bathtub swaddled with blankets and towels
soaked in urine and vomit.

Army Brat on Oahu, 1980-1982
By Melissa Ridley Elmes

In Hawai'i we lived on Halawa View Loop hibiscus growing behind our Army base apartment building now long gone a ghost torn down aloe plant at the bottom of the stairs we picked it fresh on our way to our fifth-floor flat home from Bellows beach to soothe our reddened arms and legs rubbing the slimy coolness from within the thick stem on our faces on one another's backs after

A day battling jellyfish in the surf those painful ghosts floating in the shallows but if you swim too far out to avoid them the water beckons you further further sometimes it takes an hour to get back to shore even when the shoreline seems so close and I feel that knot of fear *what if I can't get back what if I drown*? but I never drown and fear never stops me from diving deep again into

That water brighter blue-green more aqua more marine than Crayola or Prismacolor could ever manufacture it compels me more lovely than siren's song the song of the deep the song of the waves of the whales I know are out there but never see swimming low below the dolphins flinging themselves with abandon out of the water shining silver in the morning sunlight

There is nothing to stifle the noise no barrier between beach and ocean and sky no muffling like the fog the snow that traps all sound cradling the world winter white and silent on the mainland; here at the island-edge hear the waves crash break on the beach hear the birds calling hear the wind and the sun calls too if you listen closely enough you can hear the warm

Smell the salt on the air feel it on your skin water and sand baked into your arms by the sun hardening into a gritty briny layer like your own animal shell sensory overload sensory repletion there is nowhere anywhere else so loudly so proudly what and where it is as this beach at the edge of the world *look at me listen to me smell me feel me taste me*

My sister and I take in that beach those waves feel the smooth and sharp of empty shells between our fingers feel the warm dry sand of up-beach the wet cool sand of down-beach between our toes the swirling of green-blue water around our children's legs the splat of the foam boogie boards against the surf of the waves against our faces every sense acute on duty wholly engaged

Building shapes in the sand dinosaurs always dinosaurs burying one another to our chests breaking free like Superman drinking lemonade eating cheddar burgers charred on a hibachi grill watermelon gritty with sand from our hands that we can never get off no matter how many times we dip-swish them in the shallow waves splashing playfully flinging salt water at one another

Stop it our mother calls *stop it and get in the car* as the sun slides down toward the water and the blue all around us dims our father douses the charcoal with water from our buckets packs up the grill the cooler while we flap our towels in the wind releasing the sand sending it skittering sometimes into one another's eyes sometimes crying sometimes laughing always replete then an

Afternoon sunshower liquid light falling rain dropping from the sun-drenched sky like fiery stone chunks blown from a volcano on the Big Island a *National Geographic* cover photograph sprung to vivid life; again pay attention to the bright hibiscus behind our apartment beckoning begging to be picked to be worn in my hair to be made into a lei worn around mom's neck

The weekend flows into the school week like waves onto the beach like lava sliding along well-worn paths ridges formed year after year after year all the Army kids go to the same school Red Hill elementary where we learn lessons about the formation of the islands learn about Hawai'i's entry into the United States learn about King Kamehameha learn about

Luaus make paper flower leis and arm and wrist bands with a beautiful native woman her hair so thick and dark her big brown eyes shining with kindness she shows us how to hula to "Hawaiian Rainbows" her movement as fluid as the gentle water swelling beyond the surf undulating under the sky and the sun in the dance of nature under her supervision we transform our clumsy child

Bodies into trees, into waves, into the breeze blowing *you must become the music you must become the movement* she tells us *you are beautiful dancers* I want to tell her *no you are the beautiful dancer* but we are not supposed to talk during lessons so I think it hard and hope she hears my thoughts after the luau morning lessons learning cursive then lunch then

Red dirt on the hem of my yellow sundress and on my knobby pale-skinned knees and on my fat little feet bare after lunch flip flops kicked over the fence of the elementary school playground swinging into the sky during recess spare pairs on the floor in the closet of our apartment $1.00 a pair on clearance at Aafes just down the road from Halawa View Loop

Our mother still has her favorite muumuu the coral our father harvested with his own hands both man and plant were living then now both are dead there is a painting bought to decorate the Army housing white walls they wanted to throw it away when we moved *no*

I want it please I said rosy sunrise over the water waves calling to me this relic of my childhood

Beckoning if I could climb in that frame re-enter that ghost world *I would oh I would oh I would.*

The Kiwi as Metaphor
By Gary Reddin

I wanted to say this
eat the kiwi darling
even if it stings your mouth
cut its tender flesh open
to whisper your secrets
you know it will hurt you
but you are a rebellion
burning from the inside out
searching for metaphors
in everything you taste
I hope you'll tell me
what the kiwi really means
I think I might know
but your lips hold
the only truth

We Teach High School
By Andréa Rivard

They laugh when we tell them what we do. They say, You spent all that money just to make less than $60k? And we say, Yeah, we did, but what were we supposed to do instead? Something we don't love? And they say, You can't be serious. You don't actually love your job. You just couldn't think of anything better to do with your English degree. We smile politely, used to suppressing swears and unkind thoughts about others. We do love this, we say. And they shrug and say, You must be crazy, then.

Sometimes we think, maybe they're right. We're always tired after all. We sometimes take naps during the periods when our rooms are empty, between the bell at 11:22 and the one at 12:05. (This is easiest when we're in our first few years teaching, since our bodies are still young and not yet worn.) We eat our lunches instead while circling the room, listening to conversations. Our microwaved Smart Ones meals get cold when we leave them on top of the projector in order to call all those teens to attention, to say, Hey, friends, don't forget that there are two parts to a theme: its universality and its arguability.

We do too many jobs. We are teachers, yes, some of English, some of history, some of math or science or theater, but we are coaches, mentors, counselors, parents, nurses, too. We keep band aids and tampons in our desk drawers and the number for CPS on our cell phones. We buy extra tissues and hand sanitizer during flu season. Our inboxes have unread emails from the principal, from parents, from our fellow teachers, from professional development opportunities we're ignoring, but never from students. Never from students, who are asking for more: more time on their essay, more instruction on comma rules, more after school time to sponsor a book club. And we always say yes to those things and then we add more hats to our collections. We do even more jobs we aren't exactly trained for. This is especially hard on the youngest among us, the ones who are ripe and oozing energy in August, with skin still dewy and firm. We look too much like the students, then, and they think that we are like them. They think we can do it all, and we try for them, we really do.

In the book clubs we sponsor, where they read things like *Speak* and *The Hate U Give*, we learn more about them: Miss R, what if this really happened to someone we know? Sometimes we know they're asking for themselves. Sometimes we look over their shoulder to see a friend with perked ears. In the cheer teams we coach we learn that girls *can* be friends, that they'll stick up for each other and help each other out. Miss R, I can't take that solo because Diana is better. Please give it to her instead. In Junior English, we watch their writing grow. We see them make more connections, ask more questions, use semicolons correctly. We swell with pride.

We don't ask for anything. Well, sometimes the history teachers do, and the football coaches, especially when the new fiscal year begins, but the rest of us send coupons around in the group chat in August and then again in January for school supplies, and we scour Pinterest for ideas that aren't elementary. We buy lamps for each other, notebooks, pencils, label makers so that our things don't get stolen. We share ideas for how to ensure that our favorite surge protectors (yes, we have favorite surge protectors) don't go missing and for how to keep students from knowing that we have stashes of leftover Halloween candy in our desks. And in February, when the supplies are low again and the piles of notebooks have dwindled down to just the ones with missing pages, we buy each other Starbucks and are more grateful than we should be when parents send their kids with $5 gift cards for us on Valentine's Day. In the lounge and the hallways after school we say to each other, My God, I wish I could help Jonny. Or My God, I wish Carrie would come to class. And we also say, But, you know, Carrie's grandmother just passed away, and now she's the one getting all those little ones to school and making sure they have at least two meals a day. Instead of asking for help we just collect together our extra pennies and make gift baskets to leave on doorsteps, or we collect together our gently-used coats and shoes and hand them out to the Carries in our classes. We do this discreetly so no one gets embarrassed, so that other kids don't find out. We secretly smile when their attendance improves.

We run all the tests that are mandated by lawmakers who forgot what the point was, who tell teary-eyed stories of that one teacher who changed their life and who they still visit, because wouldn't you know that she's still working at the same school they attended thirty years ago. Hell, when we find a district we love, we'll stay thirty years, too. We curse them like we curse the people who tell us we can't possibly love our jobs as we pace the room, "actively" proctoring AP test after state test after district test. We bring the kids fruit snacks and granola bars because they won't get breakfast and tell them to eat their brain food only at the scheduled breaks. We tell them that yes, their best effort is required and hope they'll do well, since we're getting graded on their scores.

We take cell phones and start little collections on our desks, which we return at the end of each day. We have difficult conversations in the hallways after some heated incident about why no, it isn't okay to talk to others like that, especially not your teachers. And when those teens say, Why? I don't have to respect you just because you say, we sigh and hold our hearts inside our chests and say, You're right. You don't. Just remember that I care about you, and this only works in one of five cases. There are the times, too, especially in those first few years, when we stand frozen in place because some boy has made the comment *I'm only six years younger than you* or another comes into our room during passing period to say *There's a rumor someone started that says you're going to sleep with Danny after graduation. I just thought you should know.* We don't know what to do then. We look at our clothes and assume it's our fault, that our knee-length skirts are too showy, that we must need to wear frumpy sweaters. We go back to the white board and pretend everything's alright, but we cry to each other over wine on Friday nights about how our hearts hurt, how these kids have finally gotten to us, how we feel that we've done something wrong. Is it something we said? Is it something we did? Is it something we wore or how we styled our hair? No, it's just kids. Sometimes we tell the principal, sometimes we don't. We help each other plan out what to say and what emails to write, and by Monday we're back with smiles on our faces and a room full of kids who don't remember that we ever disagreed or were hurt. We continue on.

We're trusted with secrets, with cries for help. Should I break up with him, Miss R? Miss R, should I ask her to prom? Should I really let him read all of my text messages? We guide them with anecdotes, we tell them we'll spy. We answer with honesty, even if we know we'll let them down. We've practiced this. We've sometimes been wrong. We consult with other teachers when the questions seem hardest or funniest. In the lounge, we tell stories about their dramas, about the funny things they do, about how it was

Carlos (Carlos!) who noticed that we changed our hair, or Abby who liked our new shoes. We tell stories of how Jackson, the one who's struggled the most, had the most insightful comment today. How Pearl, the one who couldn't figure out how to link her evidence to her claim, had the highest score on her short writing assignment.

But there are days, so many days, or really, so many hours, when we feel that we can't. Miss R, what are we doing today? a bright-eyed Rosy asks, a girl who is on campus at every moment she is allowed so that she doesn't have to go home. I'm not sure, we say, attempting to avoid her, not yet ready to add her problems to our own, but I'm sure we'll learn something. We duck into the lounge to drop off our lunch and wait for Rosy to find another teacher to bother. Then, in our classrooms, we realize we have ten minutes until class starts and nothing really planned, so we decide, without too much thought, to read a front-page article from the *Times* with the kids. We sweat through our sweaters when we realize we weren't even remotely prepared to handle the conversations it stirs, that they're asking us about our politics, and we're so nervous that we tell them the last twenty minutes of class are for them. Free day? they exclaim, and we say, Yes. Free twenty minutes. Don't leave. A few leave, car keys rattling. We don't change the attendance sheet, feeling guilty that we started this whole thing. We run to each other's classrooms during our planning periods and panic-cry, but Mrs. K says, Hey, don't worry, every day is new.

And somehow we didn't align our calendars, and their literary analysis essays are due on the day of our (newly) nine-year-old's birthday, which means that we will get about five hours of sleep each night for the coming weekend since if we don't celebrate, we will hear But Mooooommmmyyyyyyy, you proooommmmiiiiiised for so long we'll cry in the bathroom, and if we don't grade these essays this weekend we won't have the data we need for the team meeting on Monday. But we choose our own children, and we come to the data meeting with one small stack of a good variety of papers we did get to. We can still prioritize under extreme stress and lack of good sleep, right? (Of course, when we grade the rest, we realize that of the hundred and seven essays we did receive, the twenty we chose to bring to the data meeting were not the best spread, but who needs to know that? Not our department chair, that's for sure.)

In April, we get a fluke cold that has started spreading around, but we only have about ten instructional days in the whole month, and we can't afford to skip one of them by taking a sick day, so we take more DayQuil than is recommended and bring a whole box of Puffs from home and a bottle of hand sanitizer and head to school. When we start the lesson and have to keep pausing to blow our nose, one of our best students tentatively approaches us where we've stepped out yet again—one foot in the door to ensure we're still watching—and says, can I help you run this today? I'm actually really good at this, and you can interject from your desk when I miss something. And we say, Oh yes, please do, and we don't even bother to try to cover up for the fact that we're passing off responsibility to a seventeen-year-old, and they take the lead admirably, and we realize that, actually, we might have been able to leave them with a substitute. They would have been alright.

But that's not exactly what the gradebook says, and that day we do take off to go to a PD seminar the principal recommended, makes us feel like they'll never recover. But they will, and, somehow, we get kids to pass. Somehow, we celebrate. We go to graduations and cry big, gulping tears when that kid who scraped by with a D+ last year and C- this year walks across the stage and finds our eyes in the crowd. We talk with anxious and excited guardians who thank us for helping their kid get into the college of their dreams. We seek out the parents of those who are going to trade school to make sure we can cry more tears and say, You'll never believe how proud we are.

Then we go off for the summer and learn some more. We sit in hot classrooms in our shorts and our school t-shirts, and we listen to someone say, Hey, you know, there's something else you can do: you can scaffold your lessons differently, you can create mini-teams, you can track data in this new way. We inwardly groan but outwardly say, Yes, tell us more about the more we can do, and they oblige. We wonder if we'll ever learn to say no. We pretend that we're only sweating because of the room, because the air conditioning only gets turned on when there are kids in the building (and, actually, it doesn't work in this classroom anyway), but really, we are sweating with the thoughts of *Will we be enough? Will we do enough? Will our families still see us, even if we add on this new thing?*

When the back-to-school nightmares start, the ones where we start an R-rated movie and are called out of the room, the ones where we have made no plans at all and arrive three hours late, that's when we question. Why *did* we spend all that money to make less than $60k? We share some answers in the group chat, answers that read like dedication pages: For the teachers who taught us, who gave their all so that we could learn. For that feeling in our chests when their faces light up, when they're filled with ah-has. Because we went unseen as kids ourselves. Because we didn't go unseen. Because someone stirred our passion for language. Because we were encouraged to pursue our dreams. We ask the young ones in their newly acquired classrooms, why are you here? And they say things like, Because my seventh-grade English teacher changed my life, or Because I can never let another queer kid feel that no one cares. There is always something deeper, something they quietly hold, and we know: we are driven by our own traumas. We are driven by our students' light.

There's always something, though, that eventually gets to us. For some it's yet another personal essay about abuse at home. For some it's the funding. For some it's the workload after someone else quit or some other programming got cut, or just the original workload because we're all teaching at least three preps and doing lunch duty. For some it's something bigger, something political or cultural. But when it hits, we think we might've found it, our limit, but our spouses and partners remind us that, like all good things, there are dark patches, and it can't, possibly, last forever. We try in these moments to remember the fire we used to feel when people would say, You can't be serious. You don't actually love your job. And the longer we do this, the more we give of ourselves, the more often we think, maybe they're right. But what are we supposed to do instead?

Cleaning Up This Town
By Florence Murry

I will clean my kitchen drawers.
I will keep away the faces that stared out

from the pages of the NY Times on a damp March morning.
I will fold towels in thirds, put them in a basket and push

them back into the closet to vanish the images
of children killed by guns. I will hall gravel to the planters,

and pour pebbles over the soil bag after bag to cover faces—
infant brother in his crib, a gun left in an open dresser,

the five-year-old in the back seat of a Mustang, the gun
left between the seats. I get on my hands and knees to scrub grout,

to scrape away the century old rifle under my son's bed.
The gun my grandson loaded with one bullet and pulled the trigger.

Selected Poems by Michelle Ott

On Knowing

I didn't always know.
Well, really, I did, but not
in the way you're supposed to.
How was I supposed to come out
of the closet, spectacularly sure,
when I didn't even know I was in
a closet at all?
Until I was nine,
and then,
(and sometimes still
now)
it was a curse, the L
word, not a word
to let linger
on your lips
the way my eyes
linger on hers.

I still hate saying the L word.

What good is it to know
myself when she speaks
in a foreign tongue?
How am I supposed to paint
a self-portrait
when there is no reflection?
If a tree falls inside of me
and I cannot recreate the sound
it makes as it sends ripples whipping
through the gaps between my ribs,
then was the tree ever really
there?

My first kiss was with a girl
named Lindsay
on the stained shag ocean
that carpeted my basement.
We were eleven.
I was twenty-two
when I realized
she counted.

Moon in Leo

When my tiny lungs first took
that breath of sterile air,
Artemis did not bless me
with the gift of self-sufficiency.
She bent down to kiss my tender,
bloody brow, afterbirth on Her lips
and teardrops salting mine. I have not stopped
wailing since the womb. I clutch
to crutches and rest the weight
of my heart on strangers' shoulders. I am radiant
but fleeting, burning through
matches to stay alight. I am abundant
yet empty, a porcelain tea cup with a hairline
fracture, intricate and delicate and desperate
for a river's love to keep me full. Goddess,
You made my arms too short to reach across my chest.

The Raccoons in Riverside Park
By Kat Stubing

Resemble voluptuous cats
Slinking around the grassy hills and
Cuddling in hideaways within the great wall

Have you seen the tiny one
Peeking out from behind her mother's
Protective grayscale tail just enough to study

The humans taking their photos
While leashed dogs whine anxiously to
Continue walking alongside the choppy Hudson

I spot her right away and think
Of you and how I wanted to be the fur
That wrapped around your little body as you took

Your first look around the world
Full of wonder and inquisition so much
So that you yearned to take a bite out of the sky

Two bosomy felines climb the
Stone wall to harvest the pizza crusts
Left for them by a crinkly woman in navy robes

By the time I look back that
Wide-eyed kit has disappeared and
I am reminded of my propensity for distractions

Ministry
By Gary Lark

Sometimes I feel like Balaam's ass,
able to see some apparition, some vision
of the truth standing in the road
and it bothers me. Truth, I know,
is a slippery eel. Try to grasp it
and it slithers away,
or it changes into a porcupine.
Can you have faith without truth?

Clara and I came to Cline Valley
after serving fourteen years
in a lively church in Sacramento.
It was busy enough to keep me
from thinking too much.
There are similarities: bottom line,
people want to know they are saved,
that they are on the path to heaven.
A little assurance, all that's needed.

I keep pointing out places of symbolism.
I can talk about history connected to Revelation,
the language used to keep the authorities at bay,
like Soviet writers telling science fiction stories
to keep from being sent to Siberia.
Then I'm asked about the End Times.
They want to know what it says
so they can sit at their chicken dinner
knowing they will be swept up
to be with the Lord while their neighbor
serves centuries of torment.

Knowing, that's the problem.
They don't want history or metaphor,

they want to know the end of the fairytale.
Okay, I said it. Blasphemy.
I can sincerely pray at someone's bedside,
but bible study follows a pattern—
that history stuff is interesting
but how can we tell the future?
I try to talk about the Word
being a guide for living, now,
that the future will take care of itself,
disappointing many.
It appears I'm becoming the porcupine.

In school I remember debating God's existence,
being assigned one side or the other.
Starting out, every question had an answer;
later, every answer had a question,
until we hovered in the ether between.
Arguing whether or not many churches
follow Paul rather than Jesus.
What is worship?
Is God the universe or the whisper
that brings all out of nothing?
A Hebrew God talking with a Greek accent.
Boiling scriptures down to essence.
Looking behind burning bushes.

What if the Asians are right?
That we live hundreds or thousands
or millions of lives, that God whispers
through a matrix of some evolving?
Sometimes I think we touch the elephant
convinced we understand a pineapple.
We look at the edge of darkness
and see our ignorance.

There are few folks willing

to dive into that opaque water,
most want to bless the sausage
and pass the mustard.
I have trouble filling words with meaning.
Do they know? Or care?
Clara thinks it's my job, our job,
to do what is asked.
She may be right, often is,
but I long for retirement
where no one thinks I have an answer.

During the Taurus Moon
By Nic Sattavara

leave left. count beetle rummaged

leaves. find the tallest tree. husk

a weathered bough. face north

west. draw out your oils

with smoke. braid cedar or sage in

the pit of a fallen branch. meditate on

meditation. forage inland.   for

acorns. bury their fruiting   bodies

at the roots of the oldest   trees. weep

for the loss   of bees.

dye twigs with wine.   drink &

choral your lore to these soils for

another night.

always on trial
By Abbie Doll

my life is spent in a stale cramped courtroom
day in and day out, a series of complicated hypotheticals
prompts me to prep and perfect my defense
a statement I'll never need but always have prepared
my energy is wasted, thrown at a trial that never seems to come
in my brain lives a judge—operator of everything behind the scenes
conducting my every move, settling my eternal fate with his
splintered gavel
I listen for his inevitable verdict
echoing like a resonating shot in this otherwise silent room

The Fire Escape
By Christopher Milligan

Annie's sisters busied themselves in the cluttered kitchen after the memorial service, moving purposely from task to task. In the living room, Stephen could distinguish bits of their hushed conversation as they rummaged the pantry, drawers and cabinets for this and that. The rest of the adults were tangled in knots of three or four debating the course of his life without Annie and the kids. "He's young and strong," said a co-worker. "Give him time." "Losing your wife and kids like that is too much," a neighbor clapped back. "The survivor's guilt alone is a goddamn mountain." Meanwhile, the young grievers escaped the adult death banter that had taken on a life of its own, choosing instead the calm of quaking leaves and the privacy of the treehouse Stephen had built for Declan and Lily in the massive sycamore centered in their tiny backyard.

The afternoon's long shadows marked the end of the wake. The leftovers were neatly wrapped, labeled and stored in the refrigerator. Stephen walked around the quiet bungalow, stood in the doorway of each room, and like a guest, awaited an invitation to enter. The house had morphed into nothing more than bricks and mortar, the transformation surreptitious and cold. He decided to move. He would remain in Indiana, but not in Seymour. Though he would miss the familiar sweet smell of his family, the weight of all it conjured would have been unbearable.

Stephen settled on a move forty-five miles south to the southern Indiana town of Madison, on the banks of the Ohio River. Forty-five miles was far enough away to secure the anonymity he needed to avoid the questions about how he was doing and the well-meaning assurances that everything would be okay. He understood that if the weight of losing Annie and the kids didn't crush him the heavy doses of small-town pity would. After two days of buzzing through humdrum townhouses and rear cottages on squishy back-lots, Stephen agreed to look at a third-floor apartment in a run-down Victorian. The realtor, an up talker with a bouncy ponytail, described the space as a hideaway in a quiet neighborhood. The scuffed wood floors, sloped walls, and exposed brick chimney gave the stuffy space a rundown quirky charm. The musty tang that seeped from every wall and floorboard did not bother Stephen. It was the fire escape, just behind the living room, which sealed the deal. He imagined hanging out on the rusted iron mass with stubborn pigeons, studying the ebb and flow of the neighborhood in anonymity, a cigarette in one hand, a mug of coffee spiked with whatever in the other. "This will do," he told the young woman.

The garret remained mostly bare except for a small spare room with a large window. The crumbly concrete windowsill was randomly dotted with pigeon shit, like an abstract acrylic. Stephen kept a small desk in this space where he'd sit for hours, surrounded by the kind of clutter that grows when something else goes missing.

On the west side of the garret, two small windows gave view to St. Rosalia's worn teeter-totters, swing sets and a singular chain basketball hoop, set against the silhouette of the church. One large bell rang out each day at noon followed exactly fifteen minutes later by children flooding the asphalt play area. Stephen especially liked to watch the play time after lunch and then later when parents and buses lined up to chauffeur the future back home for safe keeping.

It was the time of each morning when the neighborhood gushed with beginnings that Stephen would reluctantly lean into the day and watch the young couple across the street. She always slow walked her handsome partner to the curb and punctuated her "goodbye-I-will-miss-you-kiss" with a hand on each side of his face. He always returned the affection with a hug that buried her in the lay of his chest.

Night always came around too soon, slogging Stephen's memory indiscriminately. It was always the same, maddening in its constancy. They were off to the last football game of the season. Annie plopped in the driver's seat with Lily's pink and orange scarf, pushed a clump of Lily's unruly auburn hair behind her tiny ear and then chanted, "Are we ready for some football?" Declan was wearing a dirty White Sox cap—it was too big and perched sideways. He pinched Lily, who had wrapped the pink and orange scarf around her neck in a humorous attempt at chicness. She squirmed and begged Declan to stop pinching. He ignored her the way ten-year-old boys ignore their little sisters. Annie looked at Stephen, squeezed his hand and rolled her hazel eyes in one of those front-seat-side glances that only parents exchange. Stephen complained that they were running late and that he didn't want to miss the kickoff. Annie winked, kissed his cheek and suggested he drive instead. Twelve blocks later, a delivery truck blew a tire and ran a red light. Stephen can't remember if she let go of his hand.

Life from a distance held some advantage given Stephen's state of disrepair. Observing the cursive flow of people in motion reminded him to at least eat and breathe. Their stories lived in his imagination and carried him from one point to another in the claustrophobic circumference of his new geography.

One morning, Stephen noticed a slight change in the silhouette of the young woman across the street. A kiss on her growing belly by the expectant father confirmed what he suspected. Stephen wondered which parent would settle in the role with the kind of ease children deserve. Would their child be a pianist, a writer, maybe an Olympian? Or, ordinary in those abilities by which most people are measured, but extraordinary at friendships and family? Frames of Annie smiling through the stages of her first pregnancy then holding six pounds and seven ounces of Declan, fisted and puffy-eyed, played like an old movie reel in Stephen's mind. Images of the giant sycamore, a treehouse cradled in its impressive limbs, Declan's first steps, and Lily, so tiny and quiet, flashed and then vanished. If he'd only turned right, controlled his impatience and not taken the short cut. And what if Annie had driven? Stephen took one long final draw of his morning cigarette and flicked it downward to the strip of grass pinched between his building and the one adjacent, catching the attention of a young boy throwing a tennis ball against an old shed.

"Hey, mister, you shouldn't smoke!" the young boy called up to Stephen. "You new here? I'm Cian."

"Moved in a couple of months ago," Stephen said over his shoulder as he raced up the fire escape three steps at a time.

"Know anything 'bout baseball?" Cian shouted with cupped hands. Stephen closed the door, breathless from the encounter, not the stairs.

He had been a good father and husband. Everyone said so. But with Annie, Lily, and Declan gone, this assurance meant nothing. His job as a finish carpenter paid well and allowed Annie, a watercolorist, to explore her passion, plus afforded him the kind of schedule that made family time easy to come by. The summer before the accident, Stephen added Little League coach to his schedule. Declan became his shadow and Lily developed a fondness for hanging around the dugout, a habit Stephen quietly enjoyed and Declan openly hated. But it was always Annie, with her effortless way, they turned to for advice on friends, crushes, and the teacher who they were certain had it in for them. Stephen, with the tape measure that took up residence in his back pocket and a carpenter's pencil always wedged between his ear and temples dusted with gray, was the go-to for fixing bikes, building tree-house furniture, and coaching baseball.

Stephen's privacy, not to mention his morning routine, had been invaded by the little boy. He wasn't annoyed by it. He just wasn't sure he was ready for it. If Cian was anything like Declan, he had probably already forgotten about their chance encounter. Stephen was surprised to find the young boy standing outside early the next morning. He was holding a yellow tennis ball in his right hand and examining it like a curious pup.

"Keep the ball on your fingertips, not in the palm of your hand. It's Cian, right?" Stephen always began each Little League practice by describing how to hold a baseball. He was taken aback by this force of habit that he was certain had died along with Annie and the kids.

Cian nodded enthusiastically, then spelled his name twice for Stephen's benefit. "Like this?" he asked as he thrust his hand in the air for inspection.

"Your grip should contact all the seams at once. I know it's a tennis ball but the seams aren't much different from a baseball."

Cian fumbled with the tennis ball. "Like this?" he asked and stood on his toes, reached out his arm and rocked his hand back and forth.

"Better. You'll get used to it," Stephen mumbled through pursed lips, balancing a fresh smoke. "Practice holding the ball a little every day and you'll know what I mean."

Cian posted a crooked grin. "See you tomorrow?"

"See you tomorrow, Cian."

Neat stacks of condolence cards and notes stood in contrast to the messy surrounds of the spare room. Those having a personal note along with a memory of Annie or one of the kids were kept in a decoupaged shoe box, a school art project and Father's Day gift from Lily. A photo of Declan and Lily in the dugout slipped out of one of the cards from the grandmother of one of Declan's teammates. Stephen smiled at their silly pose then began to open unlabeled boxes in rapid succession. *Annie would have labeled the goddamn boxes*, he mumbled in frustration. Two heaps, seven boxes and one cigarette later, a trace of sweat, mink oil, and leather revealed the identity of what Stephen had been looking for. He brought the soft old baseball glove to his nose and buried his face deep in the pocket. Suddenly it was pitch and catch with Declan. The smack of the ball in their gloves was like morse code and they didn't need to say a word.

The large bell at St. Rosalia's rang at noon, as usual, but the raggedy playground sat empty. Stephen had forgotten Easter was the following Sunday and that spring break had begun. The pale of the sky and the cool morning breeze had given way to a *peekaboo* sun, as Lily liked to call it, and with it came the familiar thump of the tennis ball hitting the wooden storage shed. With school out, Cian would be at it all week and Stephen was not in the mood for the kind of chit chat Cian offered. The pigeons, which had lined the gable like bombardiers, began their swoop toward Stephen. Distracted by the commotion, Cian, who had added a baseball cap to his look, looked up at Stephen, squinted and smiled.

"Hey, Stephen, watch this!" Cian yelled as he cupped the tennis ball and then threw it against the shed.

"It's better, but line up to your target," Stephen said. "Have your feet and shoulders in line with the spot on the shed you're trying to hit."

"Cian, inside right this minute. I mean it!"

Stephen was almost back up to the top landing of the fire escape when the same voice called out, "Are you *the* Stephen who showed Cian how to hold a baseball?" Stephen turned and nodded yes as he searched for a cigarette.

"I'm Becca, Cian's mom. Got another one of those?"

Stephen tossed Becca his crumpled pack of American Spirits with four smokes and a Bic lighter tucked inside. Becca mumbled thank you and fussed with her icy blonde hair piled in a messy twist bun.

Relaxed by the first heady pull of the cigarette and grateful for the prospect of adult conversation, Becca leaned against the side of the building warmed by the morning sun, closed her eyes and began to talk.

"Can't say the hills of east Kentucky offer much. There sure as hell wasn't much to do in the town where I grew up other than screw around and then cross your fingers you didn't get pregnant."

The throaty timbre of her drawl pulled Stephen further down the fire escape, one step at a time. She'd paused, picked at the frayed hem of her jeans, and then looked up at Stephen. When he unfolded his arms and leaned over the rail she smiled and continued.

"Guess I forgot to cross my fingers," Becca joked. "I was seventeen and boy crazy. Wasn't sure who the father was until that mop of black hair, widow's peak, and those blue gray eyes gave it away."

Becca's voice reminded Stephen of the young woman who narrated a lazy pontoon ride on the Cumberland River the summer before the accident. Lily and Declan spent the rest of the weekend camping trip saying "y'all" and "youins" even when it didn't make sense.

"East Kentucky hill country sure is pretty," Stephen said as he recalled setting up the tent at the KOA on the edge of the Daniel Boone National Forest.

Becca mumbled, "It's only pretty when you visit." She refueled her lungs with a jumble of warm April air and nicotine, then continued.

"I followed a man to Stockport, Ohio when Cian was eighteen months. He had a decent job and was easy on the eyes so I thought maybe. . . Turned out he didn't want a kid that wasn't his, so we moved back to Kentucky. Figured Cian could get to know his father. That lasted six months and then he stopped coming around. A boy needs a father, don't you think? Jesus, listen to me running off at the mouth. For all I know, you got some babies out in the world you don't want anything to do with."

Stephen cleared his throat. "Cian, that's an Irish name."

"Could be. The name didn't mean all that much to me, but it was easy to spell and most people would have to ask how to pronounce it. Never forget a name like that."

Stephen picked at the peeling black paint on the handrail exposing the rust beneath and then rubbed the back of his neck. "So how did you end up here?"

"This was as far as a tank of gas would take us. Seemed like a good place for Cian to grow up. He likes St. Rosalia's. I just wish he'd get the hang of making friends. This town has too much God and not enough single men for my taste. But I want what's best for Cian." Becca fiddled nervously with her hair as she glanced up at Stephen and awaited a reaction that never came. She walked away without saying a word, and Stephen returned to the familiar clutter of his spare room.

The box with Declan's baseball glove sat on one side of the lumpy futon smashed against the wall in the spare room. A box of Lily's, stuffed with scarves Annie knitted from yarn she'd let Lily pick out, sat on the other end. Annie's wooden art box, meticulously organized with brushes, paints, and sketch pads, was perched between the two. The boxes were positioned in such a way that they reminded him of how Annie would sit between Lily and Declan holding an enormous popcorn bowl in the neutral zone as they watched a movie. Stephen made room on the futon and sat down next to Annie's art box. Lily's box of scarves was on his other side. He placed his hand on the wooden box and told Annie he was sorry, then turned to Lily and Declan's boxes and said how much he missed them. Stephen wept until he was wrung dry. He wept for all that would forever be missing from his life and for everything he had taken for granted. And he wept because he knew that if Annie had driven that afternoon instead of him, he would be back home talking Little League with Declan, fixing a broken shutter or adding a miniature window box on one of Lily's four doll houses, and snuggling with Annie on the couch after the kids had gone to bed.

Stephen was awakened in the middle of that same afternoon by the familiar sound of the tennis ball against the shed. He stepped out on the fire escape and there was Cian practicing his throws and stance with Becca looking on. Becca noticed Stephen and waved for him to come down the fire escape.

"Guess what? Mom said she was going to buy me a real baseball mitt!"

Stephen signaled his approval with a thumbs up to Cian.

"Grab your cup and you can have some," Becca said as she held up an old, dented thermos.

Stephen went to fetch his mug and the pack of cigarettes he'd left on his desk. Declan's mitt, with an old baseball from Stephen's childhood tucked inside, was sitting on the futon next to Lily's orange scarf. Stephen picked up the glove, closed his eyes, and imagined the smack of the ball and the smile that followed when Declan and he played pitch and catch. He placed the mitt under his arm and headed back to the fire escape. Stephen paused, then gently laid the glove and ball next to the door to the fire escape, choosing instead to spend the rest of the afternoon looking at St. Rosalia's empty playground from the chair Annie had rescued from recycling and then refurbished.

The young sycamores that flanked the entrance to the school and had gone unnoticed by Stephen until that afternoon took him back to the exact moment when Annie assured him that the bungalow was the only house for them. The massive sycamore in the backyard was what she loved the most. It was just before Thanksgiving when they looked at the house. The tree had already been stripped by the harshness of November's wind. When Stephen questioned what Annie saw in the monstrosity, she described how its mottled bark was glorious against a sky without color. And how when it wakes from winter's interruption, jimmied by the warm April sun, the buttonballs that hung on all winter long will break apart and thousands of sycamore seeds launched on tufts of buttonball hairs, like tiny parachutes, will twirl to the ground, find a new home, and take root.

With the afternoon almost over, Stephen stepped out on the fire escape and watched the soon-to-be-father across the street walk up the steps to his front porch with a small bouquet of flowers in one hand and a bag of groceries in the other. An old man walked by the soon-to-be-father and hollered, "Afternoon, Michael. How's Megan doing?" It felt good to Stephen to hear their names. They were no longer strangers he watched from a distance. He leaned out over the iron mass, took in the warm April air and thought about the sycamore's buttonballs in the fall and its seeds in the spring. Stephen went back inside and picked up Declan's mitt that he'd left at the door earlier in the afternoon. He examined the glove's pocket, fingers, palm and heel. It was nothing more than a pound of leather, he decided, stitched by a machine and stamped with an autograph of a player long since gone. It needed a hand to shape it, sweat to fade it, and the heart of a ten-year-old to bring it back to life.

Selected Poems by Chelsie Nunn

Lamentation on Measurement

the moon is a hair tie
I see it everywhere I go
locks of my tiny universe
held back in its elastic phase
your face a moon to my solitary planet
we orbit the meaning of violence
our mutual thoughts gravitational
anchoring ourselves to nothing
tangible except one cruel moment
to the next

frost slows the grass

Again I'm

painfully aware my Frankenstein is showing
stitches willy nilly out here and there
one body part from my dead childhood
falls off behind me with a slow blink
eyes turn to crystal looking at you
morning fog probably keeps my wretched
stench down to a minimum
until we are inside
God, I can smell myself as
a dribble of oozing liquid
squeezes out between my grandfather's
disgusting ear for everything I never said right and
my grandmother's cheek bone
                      I should have never shared the

Sunny Delight with my neighbor
we didn't have enough money to
squander on our friends like that
I know you can see my skeletons
whether they are poking through or not
my mother's elbow ready to clock
anyone for any reason
dangles from the only ligament that
belongs to me; maybe it's just a thought
a wish inside my bicep
to be stronger than I really am
to be more myself than anyone else who made me

A Lamentation for the Lost Berry
By Patheresa Wells

your ripeness—once a thing searched for—
now open—slowly saturating the earth—with what could have been.

hands to mouth—simmered softly—
the succulent fullness of our potential—after its spilt.

The Lies We Tell Ourselves in Search of Truth
By Kristin Wong

I woke from a nightmare just now
There were bears and devils and ghosts
and worst of all
I thought I was a ghost

It's not real, my husband said,
and he went back to bed.
I wish I could sleep

I lie back down
I lie to myself all the time
The lies feel good
They are soothing and kind
Like balm on the site of
an aching tooth

Everything will be okay
The world will not burn
Someone will save us
It happened for a reason
Even the worst thing
Is part of a greater good

Each one, like taking a shot
Soothing, burning
They help you sleep
They keep you from sleeping

You Only Needed a Ride Home
By Shamon Williams

You were 16.
At a stop light.
Passenger seat.
Windows down.
Hair swept,
half wet from drool
that'd rivered across
your silk pillowcase
the night before. Two
giggles from the backseat.
Another car strolls up.
Idols. Rolls windows.
Peers. Aims for driver.
Sprays. Hits you
in the back of the neck
as you duck.

You were 6.
I was 8.
At a slumber party.
There's a cascade
of cousins passed out
on the carpet around us.

You wilt,
screams quick sanding
on your drying tongue.
You settle for breaths
pressing against the roof
of your mouth
as blood scrambles
to fill the vacancy.

Drunk on sleepiness and
sheer sugared determination,
I ask,
      Truth or dare?

You don't feel the car
run the red, the hum
of the base booming,
the nurse's blue latex
patting on your ebony.
You don't feel at all.
It is weeks later when
I visit you in the hospital.
The bullet cannot be removed.
You cannot go home.
I bid my pity from escaping
the balcony of my eyelids,
the net of my lashes.

You pick,
      Truth.
I ask,
      What's your biggest fear?

You smile at me.
I don't smile back.
I only wonder if you
are lonely in that body
of yours, wonder if
you'd be upset
with me if I freed you
from that bullet-ridden skin.

inventory (eighteen months apart)
By Loren Walker

I never counted
      the wildflowers along Highway 6 before,
uncut, left to stretch high and coquettish over the yellow lines.

I never looked
      so close for the specific green of the crops,
the spectacular stretch of flat farmland for countless acres.

For all I've missed
      I'm taking inventory of what I never defined:
maiden's tears, prairie-fire, lady's slippers.

I am writing down
      composition for the first time: how I'm made of jack pines,
spruce, birch, balsam, and fir.

I am memorizing
      the blue of the peninsula, the Scotch thistle and shades of
heather, the new wisps of gray in my brother's hair.

I am in love
      with the girls in soaked hijabs, giggling
only meters from where I'm a dancer again

in neck-high water,
      under a long-stretched sky, locked in glass sheen,
clicked apart in the wide-open expanse

and I swear there is more
      cerulean blue along the horizon
sea-green mountainscapes parallel to the shore,

and I'm rippling
      like a great reel of dyed fabric left to flow in the river,
so eager to leach all the dye from my threads

and run clean.

Selected Poems by Sophia Ordaz

The Evaporating Remnants

Daily I meet my mind at the water's edge,

    paint a landscape of my lachrymose lake,

    add a canvas to my cold vault of a gallery.

Last month the water held two-tone tinniness:

    Portland Cool Gray and lavender-tinged slate,

    gentle Janus guiding my hand—merciful intervention.

A fortnight ago the lake revealed rust-hued rumination,

    yielding Burnt Sienna and calcified copper,

    my eyes roving restless for the slightest shift of shade.

Last Sunday the water swallowed the sky, prism-like.

    Iris-descent, my gaze drank ROYGBIV

    like Narcissus downing a looking glass.

Today, the sight of the lake is too much

    for my soul to take in at once so

    I approach kneeling, eyes downcast,

    scoop the chilled lake, palm and pet my hurt,

    like an animal, shocked speechless.

I see my lines of heart, life, and fate

    clear through the colorless water.

This transparency—how could I ever recreate it on canvas?

My grip unravels, my vendetta unravels, I unravel,

returning my former helping of woe

to the collective from whence it came.

Three Glasses In

If kissing is breathing—you know,

in the way that lips and tongues merge involuntarily

and the way I was put on this Earth

with the natural-born instinct to have my mouth on you,

then fucking is eating,

seeing as after a 40-day dry spell,

I satisfy that bothersome biological craving

with the mechanical efficiency of spoon-to-mouth.

I tell myself this after the third glass:

I could fuck any stranger in this bar, and maybe I will,

but I would sooner starve myself,

than have my lips on anyone else but you.

Breaking Kayfabe
By Melissa Grunow

"I don't know what happened," he said, sitting cross-legged on my couch, his elbows on his thighs and hands up in the air in dramatized confusion. "But I love you, and I want us to be together."

He showed up dirty. His hair and beard were both long and unkempt. We had all spent months in isolation resulting from the governor's Shelter in Place order, but he had taken it as license to come unraveled. Whenever he shifted on the couch, I detected a slight odor emanating from him. If this was going to be his grand gesture, why didn't he bother to bathe first?

He gave me a bouquet of flowers and trail mix from the grocery store ("I didn't know what kind of chocolate you liked," he said), along with a card. In it, he tried to make a joke after he ended a handwritten sentence with a contraction.

"I don't get it," I said.

"Isn't that a grammar rule?"

I shook my head. "You're thinking of a preposition. In formal writing, you aren't supposed to end a sentence with a preposition," I said. "Though, that rule is rarely followed."

He shrugged. "I guess it was a bad joke." He laughed anyway.

A corner of the crowd chanted, "Apocalypse! Apocalypse! Apocalypse!" drowning out the ring announcer while a man with cherry red dreadlocks and face paint mimicking The Joker climbed onto the ring posts, balanced on the ropes, stretched his arms out wide, stuck out his tongue Gene Simmons-style, and hovered over the audience in an act of intimidation. He repeated the display on each of the turnbuckles before jumping in the ring and facing his opponent. By the end of the match, his face paint smeared from sweat and residue was left behind on all the body parts of the other wrestler that had pressed against The Apocalypse's face.

I didn't know who to cheer for because it wasn't my scene. I was only there to watch grown men dressed in makeshift costumes, singlets, or speedos put on a scripted show for a paying audience because the guy sitting next to me invited me. We were on our third date.

He was a referee for professional wrestling in the Illinois and the surrounding Midwest, and he wanted to expose me to his hobby. One federation nicknamed him the Gentleman. He even had a trading card: #30.

After the first match, I slipped out of the arena to find a restroom and then stood in a slow line to order a couple of beers.

"Did you take an Uber home? lol" he texted me after I had been gone longer than expected.

I returned to our seats instead of answering and handed him a drink.

"I thought maybe you left," he said, accepting it.

"Tempting," I answered.

*

"I thought things were good. I thought *we* were good. And then you just, I don't know, blocked me and disappeared." While The Gentleman sat next to me on the couch, my dogs and foster dogs romped in the space around us. Their exuberance and need for attention gave me something to focus on other than him.

"When the doorbell rang, I thought you were my Chinese food." It was all I could think of to say.

"I honestly didn't know how you would react. I was pretty sure you would just slam the door in my face."

I had a choice: Tell him to go away and hope that he did before my delivery arrived. The other option was to be polite, invite him in, and let him talk.

I was raised to be polite.

*

"This is my trading card." He handed it to me. It was my first time at his house, and he was giving me a tour. The card was tucked in the corner of a framed photo in his daughter's bedroom. She was with her mother as it wasn't his visitation weekend.

"The Gentleman?" I asked, noticing the nickname.

He chuckled. "Yeah."

"Why do they call you The Gentleman?"

"I don't know," he said. "I guess because they think I'm polite and nice."

"Kayfabe" is the impression that the characters performing and the storylines they are portraying are real. It's a sort of professional wrestling code. To break character while in the ring is to "break kayfabe." The act of breaking kayfabe is called a "shoot," and is frowned upon because it can quell fan enthusiasm and effect promotors' business.

"Are you?" I was teasing him. "Nice and polite?" So far, he had been to me. For him to be anything but a gentleman would be for him to break kayfabe.

"I try to be," he said.

*

"Would you like a beer?" I had the feeling he intended to stay a while.

"Sure," he said. "Thanks."

I disappeared into the kitchen to grab two beers out of the fridge. The doorbell rang.

"Do you want me to get that?" he called from the living room.

"No," I said as I passed through the space. "It's my dinner."

I brought the bag of Styrofoam takeout containers inside and set it on the kitchen counter before returning to the couch. I handed him his beer and took a sip from mine.

"Look," he said. "I love you. I want to be with you. What do we need to do to make this work?"

We. As in, us together. I didn't have an answer for him because there was no *we* anymore. There had only been *me* for the past few weeks, and I liked being alone without his demands for my time and attention, criticisms of when I didn't meet them, fights over text, name-calling, accusations, dismissals.

"I don't know if that's possible," I said. "We don't have anything in common." It was the easiest answer.

He tossed the ball to Meg, the German shepherd dog I was fostering. She scrambled into the kitchen and nudged dining chairs out of the way to retrieve the toy.

"Are you going to eat?" he asked. "I already ate, but you shouldn't let your food get cold."

In the kitchen, I dished up a small plate of General Tsao's Chicken. I opened the other container and found that I had ordered wontons by mistake instead of Crab Rangoon. "Do you want some wantons?" I offered. "I'm not going to eat them."

He accepted and devoured them twice as fast as I consumed my own dinner. I wasn't hungry anymore.

*

After the first few weeks into our relationship, we rarely went out. We rarely went anywhere. Our time together was most often spent at his house since he had his daughter two nights during the week and every other weekend. He would watch reruns of pro wrestling, nudging me to look up from the book I was reading or the puzzle I was putting together with his daughter to "Check out this throw," or "Watch this strike," or to bear witness to the spectacle of wrestlers entering an arena while the ring announcer introduced them with exaggerated bravado and charisma.

Eventually, his daughter would whine, "Can it be my turn?" as even she grew tired of wrestling after a while.

He would turn on a show or a movie that she loved, knowing it would hold her attention, and she wouldn't come looking for us. Then he would gesture me to follow him upstairs to his bedroom where he would bend me over his bed, enter me dry, and fuck me until he came.

*

"There are all these wrestling shows that want me to referee, but they're during my visitation weekends," he said. I suggested switching visitation weekends with his daughter's mom, but he insisted she was unwavering. Even the suggestion could result in them back in family court to grapple over custody arrangements.

Instead, he usually asked his dad to stay with his daughter when shows were out-of-town, but said he felt bad returning home so late, forcing his dad to stay up and then drive home.

"You don't have to do them," I said. "Aren't there others that are local?"

"Yeah, but these are bigger venues and bigger names, which draw larger crowds."

"Why does it matter so much?"

"I could be on TV!"

It was contradictory, this desire to be seen on the public screen because he was so insecure about his weight and appearance.

"I gained fifty pounds since last year," he said.

I knew what I wanted to say but didn't. As someone who has suffered my own bouts of body dysmorphia, I wasn't going to shame another for their own.

He never hesitated to shame or criticize me, however.

"I think you have a drinking problem," he said in response to me wanting a drink or two with dinner.

"You can't handle more dogs," he said when I took on another foster.

"You don't manage your time very well," he said when I couldn't see him every day of my Christmas break because I had woodworking orders to finish.

*

On Valentine's Day, I threw an axe at a red paper heart with his name scrawled on it. The axe pierced his name and split the heart in two. We had been broken up for two weeks. I attended the event with a friend who said she had never liked him. We were each other's single support group that night.

When the axe hit the board, both teams erupted in cheers.

I took a picture and posted it in good fun. He found a way into my Instagram, took a screenshot, and sent it to me with a threat that he was filing a personal protection order against me, for now he had reason to fear for his personal safety. I felt pinned, my shoulders held to the mat for the three count: *One! Two!*

I thought about saying nothing, but I knew his harassment would turn relentless. As someone who'd had personal protection orders filed against him at least twice by his ex, he knew the process. "It's a fundraiser for the animal rescue," I responded. "Ax Your Exes. The boards are full of those red hearts with people's names on them. Each one is a dollar donated."

"A fundraiser? Oh, okay. Cool."

Was he backing down? Giving up? How quickly my pinfall had shifted to his submission.

*

The rules in performance wrestling are loosely defined and rarely enforced. Often, as part of a show, a coach will distract or taunt the referee, so his performer can do something illegal that titillates the audience. Realistic and painful-looking maneuvers are called a "sell," and the distracted referee cannot make calls on the moves that look like they did the most damage.

I have seen this happen during a show. Afterward, I asked The Gentleman, "What were you two yelling about?"

He grinned. "Nothing. It was all part of the sell."

*

His daughter chose me to read to her before bed. She had been doing that a lot lately. I couldn't remember the last time he had been the one to accompany her upstairs and discover what She-Ra and her friends were up to on Etheria.

When I returned to the living room, he told me he had unlocked my phone.

I felt sick. "You what? Why?"

"To see if I could. I watched you unlock it earlier, and I thought I caught the passcode. So I tried it."

He didn't understand why I was angry. He didn't understand why I left.

I wasn't even home yet when the text message alerts full of disavowal started.

"Yeah, so I unlocked your phone. So what? Get a stronger passcode if you don't want me to unlock it."

*

He was scheduled to referee a wrestling show in town, and he asked me to bring his daughter. It was his weekend with her, but he couldn't say no to a gig.

I didn't want to, but I complied anyway. I picked her up from his parents' house and arrived at the venue in an area I had never been to before. He met us at the door with our tickets that he got for free.

There were four rows of seats on each side of the ring, and we were in the last row on the side closest to the DJ's speaker. It was so loud that my head hurt even before the show started. There was a cash bar, so I got the two of us bottled water. I really wanted a beer, but I wasn't allowed to drink around her. That was his rule.

There were multiple referees, so he wasn't in the ring for most of the show. I caught sight of him wandering around the venue, his wide hips sashaying in his too-tight black pants, his black and white shirt tucked in and accentuating his overhanging stomach. Occasionally, he wandered over to us, caressed my back or squeezed my shoulder, but just as quickly, he walked away, and I was left alone to care for his daughter.

I was bored. I played a game on my phone when he wasn't in the ring.

"What are you doing?" his daughter asked. "Can I play?"

"No," I said. "Watch the show."

When her dad was in the ring, he moved around and watched the maneuvers. When a wrestler went down, he fell to his knees and slammed his hand onto the mat while he called out, "One! Two!" The wrestler got up before he got to three. The Gentleman faced the DJ booth and shouted, "Two!"

His daughter was captivated. I found the aerials, body slams, fat men landing butt-first on another's chest violent and juvenile. "One! Two!" she mimicked and look at me with two fingers up. "Two!"

I couldn't help but to laugh. Her enthusiasm, at least, was amusing.

The Apocalypse was there and gave the same pre-show performance on each of the turnbuckles he had done in the other show I attended. He was repetitive, but as the perpetual heel— villain—at least he never broke kayfabe.

The final wrestlers of the night were two women: one local and one show headliner who had traveled in from a much bigger city. The local woman wore a T-shirt and bike shorts with tall socks that had self-made tassels hanging from them. The headliner was in full hair and makeup in a pin-up girl body suit. Their performance included a lot of transition holds in which the local woman had to reposition her hands on the headliners thighs so she could be picked up and slammed on the mat. They were clearly rehearsed and amateur in their execution.

The Gentleman was refereeing, and he shifted along the ropes to watch each catapult and atomic drop. At one point, they both got outside the ring, and the headliner slammed the local woman into a folding table.

"Can we go over there?" the daughter asked me, and I nodded. There was a crowd gathering to watch the shoving and grabbing. The Gentleman was yelling at them to get back in the ring and pointing toward the now-empty seats in the way a dad would do when he was scolding his own children.

The headliner won, but she held up her joined hand with the local woman so the crowd could cheer for their hometown favorite.

It was over. Three hours past his daughter's bedtime and long past the time that I was ready to leave. We waited for The Gentleman to collect his things, so we could walk out together. Various wrestlers and show crew said goodbye to him as we headed toward the door. He introduced his daughter to each of them. She grew shy and didn't answer any of their questions except with a nod or a headshake. I hung back and was introduced to nobody.

*

"Let's sit outside," I suggested. "The dogs can run around and work off some of their energy." I was grateful I had five dogs in my house to focus my attention, but I was also nervous to have them around him. Although he grew up in a small house with five German shepherd dogs, he had been both affectionate with mine but also mean. When my medium-sized mixed breed dog had jumped into his lap, he grabbed her by the scruff and slammed her into the couch, pinning her head to the cushion. Once he picked up a small foster dog from behind. Oliver was startled by the grab, and he squealed and twisted, scratched and nipped to get away while I ran up from the basement saying, "No! No! No! No!" The Gentleman held the little Cairn terrier out at arm's length and dropped him about four feet onto the couch like a mat slam.

The scratch on The Gentleman's neck was barely an abrasion. When I reminded him that Oliver came from a hoarding situation and wasn't used to being handled or picked up by strangers, The Gentleman scoffed and told me I can't handle being a foster while dabbing a tissue at his neck. In his mind, dogs were secondary. To me, they were my everything.

The only time he brought his daughter over, he let her loose in the living room where she would call the dogs, taunt them, then jump on the couch and scream whenever they got too close to her. I was in the kitchen preparing dinner and asked him repeatedly to watch her. He insisted, "She's fine," while my dogs became visibly more agitated. I finally called her into the kitchen to sit on a stool at the countertop and talk to me about school, art, toys, anything to stop her from antagonizing my dogs while her dad did nothing.

I never invited her back after that.

He always thought he was helping me with the dogs. What he never understood was I didn't need his help, and his efforts were anything but helpful. My shoulders stayed rigid as I braced myself for the worst-case scenario—a scuffle, a fight, a bite—a likely outcome of his combined ignorance and pomposity.

*

It only took two weeks for his promising first impression to fade and his reactive anger to emerge. Even so, it took four attempts to end that relationship because we grieved the absence of each other each time.

"Why didn't you offer to pay for dinner?" he asked after he had offered to take me out. I had spent the time to get ready, look nice. He showed up wearing a T-shirt and jeans (he rarely wore anything else) and spent most of the night scrolling and texting on his phone.

I got strep throat after three weeks together. I was being an emotionally needy sick little me, and he seemed moody. He dumped me because I asked one too many times if something was wrong. Three hours later, he apologized and asked me to be his girlfriend again. I relented.

Once, I opted to drive an hour in a winter rainstorm to pick up a foster that I had adopted to a couple who decided after about forty-five minutes they didn't want to keep him after all. I called The Gentleman while I was on the way to tell him that I wouldn't be able to go to his house that night as we had planned, and he broke up with me. What followed was a series of texts and phone calls as he got progressively drunk and scolded me for spending too much time on fostering dogs and not enough on anything that really mattered. While slurring his words, he oscillated between insults and confessions of love. Even after I picked up the dog—a loving chocolate lab that was adopted permanently a few weeks later—and returned home, the calls and texts continued for hours. When I told him he was unkind and hadn't said a nice thing to me in weeks, he downshifted into compliments. When I didn't accept them, he shifted again into attacks and accusations.

When the exchanges finally ended, there was a buzz in the air that made me dizzy. The next day, the house was quiet. My phone was quiet. I went through the morning routine of feeding and caring for the dogs before walking away from it all and going to work.

The loneliness was palpable. Three days later, I took him back.

The third break up was instigated by a tragedy. A foster dog broke through the gate to my basement and attacked one of my cats. I heard the squeal from the bathroom and raced down the steps to find the orange tabby lying on the floor and the dog hanging her head. There wasn't any blood, but he was clearly hurt. I tried to assess injuries, but the cat wouldn't let me. When I reached for him, he hissed and bit me. The dog was sent to a different foster home, and the cat eventually allowed me to touch him as he hid behind the hot water heater. After a day or two, he started walking around again, but his hind legs weren't working right. It was a few more days before he allowed me to pick him up. His body was thin, his skin sagging. What was once a chunky cat had become a thin guy in the weeks prior. Between his weight loss and his injuries, I knew he needed to be euthanized. I tried every day to take him, but I couldn't do it. My heart was broken. I knew he had suffered. I knew there was a level of cruelty to my delay, but I needed just a little more time to grieve before saying goodbye.

A few days later, The Gentleman came over. I dissociated as he grabbed my hips and dry humped me from being. My body had shut down. My limbs were heavy and numb.

When I told him what had happened, he berated me for being a bad pet owner and insisted we go to the emergency vet that very minute. I asked him to drive. He agreed but only if we took my car. I wrapped my cat in a fuzzy blanket and held him close.

In the exam room, The Gentleman took up all the available space. He hovered over the table and insisted on staying in the room, even though I wanted to be alone with my boy for his final minutes. I didn't have it in me to argue.

Afterward, he took me out for ice cream that I ate in silence and cried under the fluorescent lights of the Baskin Robbins.

Back at my house, I turned to him for comfort, and he started verbally attacking me again. I tried to explain, but he told me I talked too much while he did all the talking. He called me names, accused me of having an eating disorder, a drinking problem, and bad breath.

When I tried to talk to him about why I was uncomfortable that he had unlocked my phone, he stormed out.

We didn't talk for three days until he called me. I knew then that the only way to get him out of my life for good was to break up over text and immediately block him. It was unfair, but I was no longer concerned with fair. I wanted him out of my life.

He retaliated by messaging the rescue organization I fostered for that I am cruel, abusive to animals, and shouldn't be trusted to foster anymore. Everyone on the Board of Directors saw the message. I was humiliated. His message was in vain, though. They remembered how he had behaved when I chose to pick up a returned dog instead of spending the evening sitting on his couch. "We believe you," they said without asking for an explanation or justification. "We know he's toxic."

*

There was a wrestling house show forty-five minutes away that he was scheduled to referee. He again asked me to bring his daughter. I initially agreed but expressed concern about driving in an ice storm with a five-year-old in the dark to an unfamiliar city. I didn't feel safe, I said.

The Gentleman assured me it was okay that I didn't attend. He would ask his dad to watch his daughter. It would be fine. The assurance was a strike, though, a set-up.

The day of the show, he sent me text messages throughout the night: "The roads are fine." "They cleared the snow." "You can still make it." "Are you coming?" "Fine. Don't come."

He was furious I didn't change my mind last minute and drive out there anyway, as though I owed him a grand gesture of my support and commitment. Taking him at his word instead of reading his mind was a screw-job. I had double-crossed him.

His daughter attended and sat alone. He was distracted all night, he said. Even though friends of his kept an eye out, there was no one accompanying her.

It wasn't that he wanted *me* there. Really, he just needed a babysitter. His guilt trip was the ultimate power maneuver.

*

The final break-up wasn't a break-up at all. I had grown so fearful of his malicious retaliation when I would end the relationship, that I slipped away quietly. I changed my number, blocked his social media, and hunkered in my home during a global pandemic because I had nowhere else to go. I let the weeks pass and grew more comfortable as they did. I spent nights outside with the fireflies and crickets while my dogs played in the backyard.

The three people who knew I had cut him out of my life all asked if I thought he would just show up at my house. My best friend in Michigan even said I needed a plan for when he did. I insisted he wouldn't, that it was too much effort, too confrontational, too bold, and he was too lazy.

A month went by. My shoulders began to relax. I reclaimed my time and my space. I took naps. I watched whatever I wanted to watch on TV, but most days, the television stayed off. I read books. I talked to almost no one.

Then, he showed up. I opened the door expecting to find takeout on the porch and instead, there stood The Gentleman holding gifts and looking sheepish.

As we ate together in the kitchen, I hadn't realized how much I had missed human interaction. It wasn't even him that I missed. It was the opportunity to have a conversation with another person, to flit about and enjoy the mundane acts of everyday life: serving food, doing the dishes.

Finally, I spoke to him about us. "We don't have anything in common. You like to play video games and you love wresting." I paused. "I don't play video games, and I think wresting is just so, *so stupid.*" If he wasn't refereeing wrestling, he was watching wrestling. If he wasn't watching wrestling, he was talking about wrestling. I started to shake. Such a statement would surely ignite a knee-jerk reaction from him.

"I don't referee as much as I used to." That wasn't the point, and we both knew it.

He stayed for a few hours and left on his own suggestion. At the door, he asked if he could hug me. I obliged though I shouldn't have. It was only a few seconds but being held brought me to the surface and allowed me to breathe. I was drowning in my grief and didn't even realize it. He suggested we see each other again. Or maybe he asked. I shrugged in a non-committal way. He implied I should give him my new phone number, and I said email was fine. He guffawed and opened his mouth to protest but thought better of it. We weren't there yet, and he knew it. We might never be there again.

I tried to give the relationship a chance by agreeing to spend platonic time with him. It only took a few meet ups spread out over three weeks at the onset of summer for me to realize I didn't like him. His jokes weren't funny. His smiles were not genuine. His attentiveness toward me—rather than his cell phone—was probably exhausting. His kindness was a performance and wouldn't last.

His final words came to me via email. "Fuck off," he wrote.

In July, I started dating someone else, and I heard he was dating again, too. Even though I was never one to insist on ending a relationship on a positive note, I still felt residual shame and guilt, his verbal attacks stuck in my mind like burs. When I couldn't sleep, they would play on loop. I questioned my decisions, my behavior, my life. Even at his most angry, he had never physically intimidated me or hurt me. It could have been a lot worse, I thought.

My resolve came in September when I met someone who knew him. He had dated a friend of hers at one time. Casually, she insisted. Never in a relationship. Even so, they fought a lot just like we had. The difference was she once followed him up a flight of stairs during an argument. When he got to the top, he turned, and Spartan kicked her down the steps.

My body turned to ice as my face flamed red. All that time his anger toward me had been strictly words and abuse of emotions. I never believed him capable of violence. That's not how gentlemen behave. He may have been known as such in wrestling circles, but outside of the ring, he broke kayfabe, an action known as a shoot. The would-be storyline, the script, was tossed out for good, the illusion forever dispelled.

Selected Poems by Barbara Daniels

Shark's Tooth

"Are you broken?" Nicole asks.
I'm like a river birch—peeling
bark, precarious leaning.

I lie to Nicole about dreams,
fevers, aching scars. "Pick
a shark's tooth," she tells me.

In a deep mirror I'm a gawky
giraffe. "Reach through
barbed wire," she says.

I've had my husbands, my
lovers. I went to Sacred Well,
watched clouds shrink, quit

keeping score. I had a cot
in a basement, dirt floor,
looming furnace, clothesline

for washdays. I don't have
a will, can't choose someone
to pick up after me and sit

in my over-stuffed chair.
Nicole says stop whining.
She says I shouldn't refuse

to sing. I know love's an animal.

And so is fear. I have a shark
tooth talisman. I trust it.

The new neighbor cut down
his river birch. It used to bend
toward me and hold off the sky.

Adjectives

> *They are the latches of being.*
> -Anne Carson

As a leaf falls, its shadow
hurries to meet it on the chilled

ground. *Chilled* moves
through the bright season.

Bright unlatches. On the back
of the page where I write

I find the words *eagle, mother,*
both gone into distant

last summer, *distant, last.*
Eagles lock talons, turn

cartwheels and free fall.
It's sky dancing, courtship.

They mate in winter,
nest in the empty trees.

A Snowy Plover is the Color of Sea Foam

Birds plunge to the churning surf.
Light spreads over sand. I mastered

sleep. Mastered dream language.
Now I'm learning birds

and dunes. I study beach ants,
those experts on ergonomics,

those students of motion and time.
In the dunes, light filters in.

I stand at the thin hem of day
watching a plover so young it staggers.

It hurries over the wet sand,
as I walk out toward the sunrise.

The Year of Our Growing
By Jacqueline Garlitos

1

The first failure began at school
but comes home
right before Mother's Day
in the cupped hands of kindergartners,
small shoots that wither and die
though the expectant children's faces
shine on them daily.

2

Later the obsession of small peat pots
filled with mail order seeds:
castor, foxglove, yarrow, nightshade.
I am afraid to walk outside among them,
refuse to use the herbs that mingle
amongst all that loveliness.

3

Lately, my husband spreads black, loamy soil
across the wide swathes of lawn
that have given up to heat and dogs.
I watch as he tosses and tamps
several varieties of seed.

I no longer bother to garden,
save to pull the more egregious weeds.

I humor him with new hoses
and a fancy self-propelled sprinkler.

Each day he stands on the stone path
that slices through the yard,
shooing the birds
(the same birds I feed all winter)
awaiting an abundant burst of green.

His face is beautiful.

It has been a long time
since anything has flourished here.

Selected Poems by Kate Porch

Sitting in a Garden Thinking About Earth Overshoot Day

Hello fountain:
      gray dolphin cresting a wave.
Hello wood sorrel:
      poking up between two bricks.
Hello trees sheered like poodles,
yellow roses doused with rainwater,
Spanish moss scattered
across the lawn like tufts of fur,
root-cracked sidewalks,
twig snapping under a tire,
and train hissing
like an intake of breath through teeth.

I am not here
to ask forgiveness
      since I did not take the first bite
      of the apple,
      since I am not the orchard keeper,
      since my children
      will scrape up the glossy slick
      at the bottoms of their gas cans
      and we all inherit the rising tides
      from someone else.

I am only asking
for a while longer
      to sit in this garden
      and listen to the cardinals sing.

How to Love Myself

"How do I love thee? Let me count the ways."
- Elizabeth Barrett Browning

1. Put hands to skin, 2. hold the breasts like doeskin
in my palms, 3. forgive them for their crooked drip,
like raindrops sliding down glass,
for the tangle
of their blue-vein constellations.
4. Sing to my body's folds
and puckers, evidence
of its quiet tinkering, how it carries breath
like dandelion tufts on a breeze
to its fibers, membranes, filaments,
for the most I can do is thank it.
5. Remember my body
is only the ferry, 6. place hands
by my heart,
feel heat rise through its cloth
like a sun,
and think of my body as a candle
rolling down making way for a light,
of myself as the flame.

Selected Poems by Victoria Elizabeth Ruwi

Innate

No web weaver she,
wolf spider burrows
within sand dunes,
her inward tunnel
a deep flawless circle.

Beach grass reaches
to draw curves in sand,
bows within wind,
over time carving her
growth in outward arcs.

Little girl orbits in butterfly
dress, fuchsia wings bright,
the wand she waves
not so out of place in her
metamorphosis glow.

Heart Zip

My heart is a broken zipper
held together with safety pins.
I can still wear it; it's too
comfortable to give away
to the Salvation Army,
Goodwill, goodben or gooddan.
I'll mend it in time,
with needled percussion:
a heart all zipped up could
be snug, could still open.

Dead Man Walking
By Keith LaFountaine

1.

When Larry opened the closet door, he was surprised to see a pair of shoes tucked in the corner. Behind him, holding her clipboard and sucking on her teeth, the property manager cocked an eyebrow.

"Strange," she muttered. "I didn't think there was anything left. My apologies."

"It's fine," Larry said. "I can throw them out myself."

Turning, he glanced at the empty bedroom, at the white walls, at the popcorn ceiling. It wasn't the Ritz—hell, it wasn't the Holiday Inn—but he was ten minutes from downtown Burlington and heat was included in the rent.

"I'll take it," he said, forcing a smile on his face.

2.

Boxes and boxes and boxes. So defined the apartment. Larry swiped the back of his hand across his forehead, and it came away slick with sweat. It would take ages to get it all unpacked. He thought about Brenda briefly: her smile. Dancing in the kitchen. And then he looked down at the pale ring of flesh on his finger.

He shook his head and focused on another box labeled *books*. He grabbed it, lugged it into the bedroom, and dumped it beside two others: one containing his bedframe, ordered off Amazon, and the other a memory foam mattress.

His phone rang, a tinny chime breaking through the thin air. He dropped the box on his foot, hissed, inhaled harshly, and shook his head. Then, Larry pulled the phone out of his pocket and answered it.

"Larry, I need you to come down."

He suppressed his anger and looked down at the floor. At the ratty carpet. "Brenda, I'm not really in the mood to talk right now."

"I don't care. You remember *Ghost Town?*"

"The book?"

"Yes, dumbass. The book. You never gave it back to me, and Jeff wants to read it. Can you bring it down?"

"Brenda, I'm right in the middle of moving…"

"Just bring it down. This doesn't need to be a big production." The line beeped three times.

Larry sighed. Turning, he opened the cardboard flaps on the box labeled *books* and sifted through the paperbacks and hardcovers. Near the bottom he found *Ghost Town*. As he lifted it out, Larry stroked the cover. The spine wheezed when he opened it. There, on the opening page, in blue ink, was her note.

For Larry—the pearl of my life.

He snapped the book shut and marched out of the bedroom.

3.

Rain streaked down, slapping the cement like a petulant baby. An SUV sat in the apartment building's parking lot, clouds of exhaust puffing toward the sky. A rank odor filled the air: a combination of gunpowder and cow shit. Larry tucked the book under his shirt and crossed the parking lot.

The passenger's window rolled down, and he saw Brenda. Red lipstick, luxuriant eye shadow, a half-smile pricking up the left side of her face. Her jaw's sharp edge. The knowing glint in her pupils.

"Do you have it?" she asked.

"Yeah," Larry said. He pulled the book out from under his shirt and handed it to her.

As if completing some important deal, she fanned through the pages. Seemingly satisfied, Brenda turned and dropped it in the back seat of the car. She glanced at Jeff briefly, and he curled his hand around the steering wheel so hard the leather creaked in response. He offered a stiff nod toward Larry.

"That all?" Larry asked.

Brenda sat there for a minute, her eyes shining like she wanted to ask him how he was, or if he was eating dollar store Ramen noodles for dinner, or if he needed a hug. She looked down at the dashboard, then over at Jeff. And then those soft features turned as hard as diamonds, and she set her jaw.

"That's all," she confirmed. After a brief pause, she said, "Hope you're doing okay." And then the window went rolling up, and the SUV's taillights shone bright white. Jeff drove them away, drove them back out onto the street, and then they were gone.

Larry turned and walked back to the apartment. As he did, he glanced up at the sky. At the overcast clouds.

And he stepped right into a puddle.

4.

The shoes were soaked through, and as Larry stripped off his socks while sitting on the floor of his new bedroom, he wondered how long it was going to take for them to dry. The shoes and the socks. With a sigh he tossed the socks into the corner, where they slapped against the wall, leaving a glistening spot on the white paint.

He didn't have dinner, he was supposed to unpack everything, and he had to be at work bright and early the following morning. The people of Burlington needed their cough syrup and their throat pills and their ultra-thin condoms and their frozen weight loss meals. And he needed to ring them up when they came to get those items, all with a smile on his face.

"Jesus," Larry mumbled under his breath.

He thought about the look in Brenda's eyes, the way she'd hesitated before rolling the window up. The creak of steering-wheel's leather.

Standing, Larry fished out a pair of dry socks from one of the boxes. His shoes were still soaked, and for a moment he considered just toughing it out. But then he remembered the shoes in the closet.

What are the chances they're my size?

He opened the closet door. There, in the corner, he saw the shoes. They were dressy things, their material lacking the luster they deserved, but retaining a certain air of sophistication. Bending over, Larry grasped them and peered under the tongue. He didn't see a size listed, or any marking to denote who made the shoes.

"Must be custom," he said.

Straightening, he placed his foot next to one of the shoes. It looked big enough. Maybe a little tight in the toe, but not anything that would render them unwalkable.

"Well, here goes nothing."

He plopped his ass down on the thin carpet again. Then, he slipped on the socks and grabbed the right shoe, sliding it over his toes, hooking the back of it around his heel.

It fit *perfectly*. He flexed his toes, expecting something sharp to prod the fleshy side of his foot. But nothing stabbed at him. With a shrug, he grasped the other shoe and pulled it on, too.

Something tugged at his mind. Not physically, not his *brain*, but his consciousness. It felt like his existence was being filtered down a bathtub's drain, spiraling in a small cyclone, cycling into a glass bottle.

Swirling, swirling, swirling.

Gone.

5.

Michael Grady sat up on the floor of some shitty apartment building in the south end. He groaned and rubbed at his head. A stabbing pain sheaved the back of his brain. The white walls, the shade of eggshell. They were like a mother's hug—weirdly memorable.

He rubbed at the legs that spread out before him. Spindly things. Barely thicker than a twig with osteoporosis. Michael grunted.

As he stood, he remembered why the walls were familiar. They were missing the splotch of crimson blood, the spots of gray matter. His brains, painted there by Eddie. Or, more precisely, Eddie's friend, Gonzo.

Fucking traitor.

The pain in the back of his head lingered, a constant reminder. It would be useful. When he pushed some iron down Gonzo's throat and fed him three bullets, the feeling would dissipate. Or maybe it would after he chopped Eddie off at the waist. But not before then. No, it would be his metronome until he reached that house in the north end.

Sucking in breath was like pulling back a whiskey sour made by a heavy-handed bartender. Brutal and refreshing. A god damned kick to the teeth.

He glanced at the closet. If he wasn't mistaken, there was something else hiding in the closet. Not just his shoes, but...

Michael reached toward the closet's ceiling. Toward the small, almost imperceptible, rectangle carved into it. The hands were about as flimsy as the legs, but the fingers pressed against the rectangle and pushed through. The rectangle lifted cleanly, and he pushed it off to the side. Like some science-fiction monster, those fingers felt around the space until they grazed cold metal.

He smiled, and though this wasn't his body, Michael knew it was the same wolfish grin Marnie Jones had fallen in love with so many years before.

He pulled down the revolver and replaced the rectangle. Michael snapped open the cylinder and stared down at the six bullets inside.

"Locked and loaded," he growled.

He snapped the cylinder closed and tucked it into the back of his waistband.

6.

As he walked around the apartment, tapping his forefinger on his chin and considering his options, a sharp knock cracked through the front door. Turning, he reached his hand toward the revolver.

Moving aside, out of the line of fire, he called, "Yeah?"

"Larry?" A woman's voice. "Larry, can we talk?"

Larry. That was the poor sap's name. The twig.

"Yeah," Michael called. "Come in."

The door opened, and a woman in jeans and a black tank-top walked in. She glanced at him, and for a moment Michael was sure she could peer through him—see through the watery prisms of his eyes and notice Larry trapped inside.

Michael could feel him, buzzing around like a gnat. But he was insignificant. Whatever the lady from Oak Street had imbued his shoes with, he wasn't going to squander the opportunity.

"Larry," she said, her tone soft. "I'm—I'm sorry I was harsh before. Jeff was being a dick, and it was raining, and I just wanted to get out of there."

Dude is divorced, Michael thought. *Or separated?*

"It's fine," he said, clearing his throat. "Listen, I have to go somewhere. Get something." He glanced toward the door again, now closed. Did Eddie know about the lady? He must have. He'd followed him to Oak Street. Michael was as sure of that as he was this guy's prick size.

The woman seemed confused by Michael's bluntness. She stammered and glanced at the ratty carpet. At the eggshell walls.

"Right," she said.

"Great," Michael finished. In one smooth movement, he wrapped his arm around her shoulders, led her to the door, and opened it. Then, she was out in the hallway, her mouth hanging on a hinge, her eyes wet and wide.

"Maybe we can grab coffee? Chat. Like old times."
"Sure, sounds great," Michael said. "I'll call you."

She smiled at that. 'Great, thanks."

And then she was turning toward the stairs, and Michael was just fine with that. He had places to be.

7.

He longed for his truck, but Larry drove a Vespa. Something about that was especially frustrating, and the steady sprinkle of rain from the overcast skies didn't help much. Michael decided to walk, giving the Vespa a single kick, sending it sprawling onto its side. Oak Street was twenty minutes away, a quick walk. And Bonzo's house was closer—on Spear Street. Assuming he still lived in that shitty one-bedroom with the curved roof and the broken window out front.

Yeah, he still lived there. Michael felt it in his bones. The dumb tub of muscle wouldn't have the need to leave. Plus, he'd probably paid off the mortgage with the cash Eddie paid him. A one-time installment for putting a slug in the back of an old friend's skull.

What a god damned mess of a world.

8.

The house was indeed the same, only now it had a tire swing out front. The rubber circle hung from a length of rope, and the branch above creaked and twisted as the wind blew. Some kid was bound to crack their tailbone or their head if they took to the swing too fiercely, but that was their problem.

Michael slipped his hand around to the back of his jeans, where the revolver bulged. Nobody had noticed while he'd walked, which was a surprise, but also a testament to the regular Joe or Jane's ability to mind their own fucking business.

He remembered, from the few times Bonzo's girlfriend Stoya had cooked them dinner, that the house had a back and a front door. The front door was loud as shit, and the top two stairs wheezed like an old man sucking oxygen from a tube. So, Michael crept around the side of the house, slipping below windows, keeping his ears pricked for the slightest sound.

There was a small screened-in porch that led to the back door. Luckily, nobody was outside playing on the plastic jungle gym or riding the bikes that were caked in old mud.

Slipping the revolver free, Michael pulled on the hammer, and slunk toward the back door. As he entered the porch, the door opened, and out walked Bonzo with the dumbest expression on his face that could have been produced: all pinched lips and eyebrows, like a fish sucking on a lemon.

Bonzo eyed Michael's piece and raised a hand outward. "Woah. What's going on?" Then, after a pause. "You know who I am, buddy?"

"Yeah," Michael seethed. "I remember, B. Tell me, how'd it feel putting a slug in your friend's head?"

Bonzo's face didn't contort with surprise or confusion. Instead, he cocked his head to the side.

"Listen, buddy," he said. "I don't know what you think I done, but—"

"Shut it," Michael breathed. "Just shut it. I backed you up, B. I spoke for you. I got you into Eddie's good graces, pulled you off the street slinging H, and *that's* how you treat me?"

"Buddy, you're talkin' crazy. I don't know you."

Michael was done. He'd heard enough. With grit and anger in his throat, he growled, "Yeah you do." And then he lifted the revolver and squeezed the trigger twice.

The first bullet tore through Bonzo's cheek, ripping flesh and shattering bone. The second pierced his eye, and that was the one that sent him sprawling back. That was the one that sucked the life out of him. Hot blood steamed out the back of his head as brains splattered the screen behind him. And then his entire body folded in half like an undercooked pretzel.

Michael stuffed the gun back into his waistband and fled the porch, walking straight back, past the bikes, past the jungle gym, until he reached a peeling fence. He hopped it with ease but stumbled on the downturn. The stumble turned into a trip, and suddenly he went twisting away down a bed of wet leaves and mulchy grass, until the left shoe hooked on a branch and came pulling free from his foot.

9.

Wet whoops of terror escaped Larry's lips as he tumbled end over end, the back of his shirt slimy with mud, the front a cornucopia of pinecones, green needles, and black leaves. When he finally came to a rest at the bottom of the hill, one of the shoes clacked by him, bouncing off the curb and tumbling into the street.

His tongue felt fuzzy, and a strange aftertaste lingered in his gums: like olives mixed with toothpaste. He spat gobs of frothing spittle onto the ground beside him but didn't see any blood. All his teeth seemed firmly lodged.

Thank God for that, he thought.

But he *did* feel the prodding, cold metal digging into his back, jutting against his spine. And he hated the sensation in his gut: the one that told him *exactly* what that thing was.

A gun.

Screams exploded from the top of the hill: a warbling cry that was grating, like vocal cords being rubbed against a cheese grater. Larry scrambled to his feet, brushing the errant leaves and needles from his chest and arms. The screams from the hill got louder as he stumbled toward the curb, as he picked up the shoe. And as he limped down the road, glancing back up at the hill where the scream was spreading, now becoming *screams*, all high-pitched and deserving of a slasher movie, a new sound joined the fray: a distorted *wheee-waaaahhh wheeee-wahhh.*

Turning, Larry saw a police siren.

"Fuck," he grunted, shuffling forward. "God damn it."

The car screeched to a stop beside him, and the door banged open. A cop with a hefty brown mustache and eyes that were as dark as pools of mud stepped out.

"You lost, son?"

He wanted to lie, to conjure some alibi, some *other* reason that would explain why his shirt was covered in muck and he was carrying a revolver.

But all he could manage, in a squeaking tone, was, "No, officer."

The cop rested his palm on the butt of his service pistol, those eyes glowering. "You know anything about what just happened up there?"

"I know some lady started screaming," he admitted. Which was the truth. The last thing he remembered before the hill was putting the shoes on back at his apartment.

"So, you take tumbles down hills for fun?"

"No, officer. Honestly, I'm just having a really bad day today."

"You're damn right you are." The cop drew his gun but didn't aim it. "Get your hands up in the air, will you?"

Larry did so automatically, knitting his fingers behind his head, as he'd seen criminals do a thousand times in movies. The cop, seemingly satisfied, holstered his weapon and approached. Then, his hands were feeling up and down Larry's body, groping at his armpits, his midsection, his back...

The cop froze. And, with stunning speed, he pulled the gun away from Larry's waistband and held it in both hands like it was an antique.

"You have a permit for this gun?" he asked, tucking it into his belt. He reached for the handcuffs next to his service weapon, slipping them free.

"I'll be quite honest with you, officer," Larry said, "I have no idea."

"What's your name?"

"Larry. Larry Kehoe."

"Well, Mr. Kehoe, you have no idea who you shot just a few minutes ago, do you?"

"I—I don't remember shooting anyone, sir."

"Sure you do. Barry Waterford? Friends call him Bonzo, though he likes B better. Works for Eddie Kasgard. Ringing any bells?"

"No, sir."

The officer's lips parted in an amused grin. "Sure, bud. Alright. Why don't you slip on that shoe? We have places to be."

"I really wouldn't like to—"

"Do I look like the kind of man who can afford to piss time away? C'mon, get your shoe on and get in the back seat. Or I'll put it on myself like you're a fucking baby."

"Alright," Larry said. "Alright." He glanced at the cop's service pistol, at his gleaming dark eyes, and he lowered his body to the curb, his hands still knitted behind his head.

"Do you understand the meaning of haste?" the cop asked.

"Yeah.

"Then why're you moving like a snail with scoliosis? Let's go!"

The curb was cold and damp, and that feeling seeped through the seat of his pants. Larry glanced down at the shoe in his hand, swallowing hard. The cop still held the handcuffs. Surely, he planned to slap them around Larry's wrists the second he slipped the shoe on. But he also got the feeling that, if he didn't agree, the cop wouldn't think twice about drawing that service pistol (or maybe the revolver nestled in his waistband) and plugging two holes in his chest.

So, with a dry mouth and a parched tongue, Larry sighed and bent over, slipping the shoe over his toe, slamming the sole of his foot into place.

10.

Michael Grady's head was still spinning when he looked through the dimwit's eyes. He raised a palm to his temple and grumbled, "Son of a bitch."

"What's that?"

When he straightened his posture, Michael saw some cop standing over him. Some cop with a familiar face. Then, everything clicked back into place. He smiled, and his excitement attached itself to his heart like angel wings when he saw a beady terror swell in the man's eyes.

"You're Frank, right?" Michael asked. He stood, slapping the seat of his pants. "Eddie mentioned you sometimes. Never met you, though." He glanced at the handcuffs in the guy's hands. "I guess I wish I could have shaken your hand under better circumstances."

"What're you goin' on about now?" Frank said, but Michael watched the fear bloom like a fungus in his pupils.

"Frank, I'm really sorry, but if you don't put those handcuffs away, someone's gonna get hurt."

It happened in a flash. Frank dropped the handcuffs. They fell and clattered on the pavement like a useless toy. His hand went to his hip, to the service weapon. The buckle was flapping, meaning he'd already drawn it once, but Michael was prepared for that. As Frank's palm connected with the black butt of the gun, Michael reared his leg back and drove it into Frank's groin.

The cop's eyes bugged out of his skull, and his hand slipped from the weapon as he sagged onto his knees. His skin turned a forest-green color, and vomit bubbled from his lips and his nose. Tears stung at his eyes.

"I warned you," Michael said.

With a swift movement, he reached around, pulled the revolver from Frank's waistband, and put it to his head. The shot was quick and harsh, like whooping cough, and then Frank's brains were splattered across the pavement, a growing swell of crimson oozing out underneath his hair.

Michael stuffed the gun into his belt and stretched, rolling his neck and extending his arms. Then, he stepped over Frank's corpse, making sure to avoid the bits of white skull that had splintered across the road, and made a beeline for the car.

To hell with walking, he thought.

11.

Eddie's house sat on the end of Wabash Avenue. It was a green thing, with fresh paint and neat windows. A white picket fence ran around the length of the yard.

Michael parked the car a few houses down, leaving the keys in the ignition. For a moment, he considered taking the shotgun that was nestled between the driver and passenger's seat, but he decided against it. The revolver was faster, easier. And he still had three shots left. Plenty to take out old Eddie.

The pavement was nice and flat out this way, lacking any cracks and colored a deep black—like midnight in the North Pole. Michael wondered if Eddie paid off a guy in the public works department. How else could someone get their road paved so perfectly while the adjoining streets crumbled and cracked from frost heaves and general wear?

As he approached the green house, Michael drew the revolver and snapped open the cylinder. Sure enough, three spent cartridges and three bullets stared back. Michael dumped the empties and snapped the cylinder back into place. Then, he returned the gun to his beltline.

The fence was beautifully uniform: not a drip of errant paint or a scratch to be seen. Similarly, the lawn was impeccably manicured.

Michael made a point to kick the fence door in and to dig the toe of his shoe into the lawn, scrubbing at the green blades and marring the matte white paint.

He peered through the windows, expecting to see one of Eddie's other guys standing there—the guys that grabbed coffee and fetched pastries. But all Michael saw was his reflection.

After stepping onto the wooden porch, he rapped on the door three times, using a scrunched fist. The knocks echoed through the house, and Michael heard scurrying footsteps. Then, a deadbolt snapped, and the door swung inward.

Standing there with a confused and somewhat fearful expression, was Judy. Her pale skin glowed in the sunlight, and her fierce green eyes were as piercing as ever.

"Can I help you?" she asked.

"I have some business with Eddie."

"What kind of business?"

"Tell him it's about our mutual friend, Frank."

Judy's gaze shifted slightly, the corners of her mouth turning down, creasing her complexion with a slight frown. She shut the door in his face.

Michael waited, slipping his hands into his pockets. He glanced at the lawn, and he wondered if Eddie's kid was upstairs in his room. Maybe listening to heavy metal, maybe reading *Tom Sawyer*, maybe Googling who exactly his father was. But as soon as these thoughts germinated, the footsteps returned, and the door swung inward again.

"He'll see you in the kitchen," Judy said.

"That's fine," Michael responded with a warm smile. "I know where to find it."

Judy's eyes narrowed, but she stepped aside, and Michael brushed by her. He almost thanked her for being reasonable. He hated killing women.

The interior of the house was a maze of hallways, and Michael easily wound his way through them, passing the study where he and Eddie had played poker with Bonzo and other friends. He slipped by the bedroom where Eddie had given Michael his first untraceable gun. He passed old photos of Judy and Michael's wedding, of their son, of vacations and expressions of glamour. He walked by it all, and in a matter of minutes, he entered the kitchen.

And there, sitting at the table smoking a cigarette, was Eddie. He glanced up at Michael, and he raised an eyebrow.

"Supposedly we have some business to attend to?" Eddie asked, blowing smoke out in a gray trail.

"We do."

"I assume you're the one who shot Bonzo," Eddie continued, calm as could be. "So, what is it you want? Money? Power? You want in on this thing I have going?"

Michael gritted his teeth. "I want your head, you two-faced lying pig."

The hint of a smile twitched at the edges of Eddie's lips. "Big words for a…well, a *scrawny* man. Take a seat." He gestured at the chair across the table.

"No, I don't think I will," Michael responded. He pulled the revolver free and pulled back the hammer.

A loud *crack* roared through the house, and Michael thought, for a moment, he'd accidentally pulled the trigger. But the sound was immediately followed by searing pain in his throat. He turned, toppling, one hand clapped over the wound, the other gripping the weapon as though it was glued to his palm. Michael twisted, and as he fell, he saw Judy standing in the kitchen's entryway, both hands clasped around a black pistol, her eyes narrowed with focus, her tongue tucked between her lips.

He squeezed off one shot at her, but it went wide, slamming into the doorway. A puff of wood exploded outward, and Judy pulled a hand away from the gun to shield her eyes. But then Eddie rounded the table, and his hulking body was in full view.

Michael choked and garbled as more hot blood spilled down his throat.

Not again!

He pulled back the hammer on the gun, gritting his crimson teeth. The bullet felt like an accidentally swallowed piece of food.

He could feel it bobbing around in his broken trachea. The seconds were dwindling, but he only needed to get one final shot off.

Eddie reached a meaty hand for the revolver, and Michael fired. The bullet tore through Eddie's shoulder, and the bastard yelped like a wounded dog, jerking to the right, a hand clapping over the weeping hole. An exasperated splutter escaped Michael's mouth, followed by a spray of frothing blood, and he wrenched back on the hammer a final time.

But this time, Eddie was faster.

With a snarl, he reached down and pulled the weapon from Michael's hand. Smears of blood stained his fingers and his palm, the one holding the weeping wound, but Eddie aimed the weapon with ease.

Michael opened his mouth to spit something foul at the backstabbing traitor. But the bullet bobbed around in his shattered throat, and the only sound he produced was akin to a strangled train whistle.

Eddie sneered, and then he pulled the trigger, and Michael went spiraling away into the void.

12.

Eddie ignored the lancing pain in his shoulder as he stared down at the mangled stranger's corpse. Judy rushed behind him, her fingers pushing and prodding to inspect the wound.

"I'm fine," he grumbled. "It's probably a through and through."

She glared at the man, at the blood tarnishing their kitchen's tiles, and she let out an exasperated huff.

"Who the hell was that guy?" she snapped.

"I don't know," Eddie said truthfully. The man's face didn't register with him. If he'd ever seen this asshole before, it'd been during a routine stop at Dunkin Donuts, or while filling up at the Cumbies on Pine Street. He'd certainly never done business with him.

His gaze traveled lower, lower, down the legs, until he settled on the shoes.

Those he remembered.

"Eddie?" Judy asked. "Do we need to worry about anything?"

"No," Eddie lied. "I'll call in a favor. Get this cleaned up. For now, don't touch anything."

Judy turned, possibly to wash her hands, possibly to fumble through the liquor cabinet for a shot of tequila. Eddie continued to stare at the shoes.

There was no way.

It was impossible.

Still...

"Judy," Eddie called.

"Yeah?"

"When you have a minute, build me a fire out back in the pit."

"A fire?"

"Yeah," Eddie said. "I need to burn these fucking shoes."

Virginia Woolf on Vanessa Bell
By Stephanie Trenchard

I saw my sister once scrawl a maze of lines
with white chalk on the black door

    With white chalk she wrote on the black door
    When I am a famous painter

She was a famous painter, just not then
Then she was shy. She rubbed out the soft chalk

    The shy painter rubbed out the white lines,
    in her capable way leaving traces of marks—

capable marks—traces of her way
Once, amazed, I saw my sister scrawl white lines

Fall
By Christina E. Petrides

shadows and sunlight
sift wind-borne
yellow leaves

autumn drifts flutter
from branches arched
above tall rock walls

roots knotted on
chiseled heights
guard the stream

trickling from
warm stepping stones
to deep cool baths

where great boulders
grow blue-green
and unperturbed

Passively watching you leave
By Matthew Birch

I

Dripping
from my lips
they form a pool

Leaving
I'm not ready in time
You're shouting
not that loud it's funny
now I can open the door

Dried eyes and silence
I want to dive in again

II

I put on my coat
when the cold finds me.
I regret
wearing flip-flops and look to you
who goes barefoot.

I shout at the cold
when it doesn't leave
and look to you once more.

Back turned

you follow the clouds

III

The oil in the frying pan
heats up
It sounds like melting rain

Just this sound
for comfort
Remembering yesterday's weather.

All This Was a Nice Place Once
By Laura Rockhold

-golden root after "earth" by Lucille Clifton

once, heredity
placed its hand in this
nice earth where
a life spread. once, it
wasn't
this dry.
allium grew wild when
once, it was a softly lit
place of rain.
a brilliant and
beautiful place that also
told of carrying. yet, we are here,
using and forgetting under
this particulate irreverence. name them
all the same—
bees see what
children see in wasted
flowers calling
varicolored prayers. it's a wonder how the trees
bare it.

Golden Root Description:

"All This Was A Nice Place Once" is a golden root; a new poetic form I created and named after its two sources of inspiration: Terrance Hayes' golden shovel, and Lucille Clifton's poem "roots." Similar to a golden shovel, the golden root uses every word of the source poem; yet, it is different in that the source poem encases the new poem. Specifically, the last word in each line (top to bottom) is the first half of the source poem, and the first word in each line (bottom to top) is the second half of the source poem. The source poem holds the new poem. The new poem lives within the source. The golden root serves as a conduit for the spirit of both poems.

Selected Poems by Nikki Ummel

Leave Taking: A Bop

How'd we get this way? Dinners on the couch,
bowls of words we swallow, bed edges hugged,
Five AM alarm hush to vacate the bedroom,
eyes trail doorways, ears cock for floorboard squeak,
tire squeal. Before our vows, we tied two ropes,
machete sliced the knot free. It frays on the mantle.

Our tongues forget *I love you*. Our conversations go silent.

My turn to rise early, I slip socks over my feet
to silence the creak of our bargeboard house.
The sun splashes your sleeping frame, peace I gulp
from the hallway. Remember how we rolled marbles,
placed bets on who could avoid collision?
You once told me you could do better, and I agreed. Now
I hoard you like canned peas. I've always lived for the future,
my darling. I thought you knew that.

Our tongues forget *I love you*. Our conversations silent.

I've thought about when you leave me. Will you again forget
the broken zipper on your skinnies, flash me parting glimpses
of your boxer briefs? A clip of jasmine in your back pocket.
Fuck, did I pluck and preen in our early days,
led you to believe we would be okay.
I'm sorry for lying.

Our tongues forget *I love you*. Silence.

Self-Portrait with My Sister's Will

I.
Last Spring
my sister called.
Phone pinned between
my ear and shoulder
I heard, *We listed you*
as Elah's guardian.

The compost crumbled
in my hands, fell in soft
sucking plops, bombing
my baby tomatoes
into trembles. *Are you*
sure? I asked. Set
my gloves aside, and rose

to lean against the
papaya tree, its soft bark
pressing into my spine like
my sister's hands once did
when we used to play
cops and robbers.
She always let me get away.

Yes. Her stern hard voice.
My response, *O-*
kay, a glass bowl breaking,
splintered, sharp.

II.
Since that day, I find myself
imagining the future:
A four-year old pulled from
the smolder of bent aluminum.

It will happen slow.
No. Maybe tragic-fast.

Too quick to buy a second bed.
So we will sleep in layers,
my body a foundation
for her small frame.
Between us,
not enough sheets,
the bed shrinks.

When she's sleeping,
I will slip from our bed
to rub clean Honeycrisp apples,
pack fruit gummies and rainbow crackers,
the companions for her
new daycare. No.
Her new elementary school.

We'll twist her hair, clip in
pink plastic butterflies,
revel in their noisy clinks,
young girl as wind chime.
Pin feather poufs over each ear.
Someday, maybe,
she will forget and

call me *Mommy*. But when
the tears come, she will
smooth my tangled hair
and tell me *hush*.

A Mother on the Eve of Her Child's 15th Birthday

In the rain, in the car,
               I wait outside
                   your best friend's house.
               You come out, beaming.

I cannot hear
               what you call back to her,
                   over your shoulder
               as you trudge toward me
but your face shines.

You climb in without a word.
I do not turn the radio on.
               We sit in thick silence, inch into traffic
         as rain smears the windshield.

I want to reach across the console and
         press you to my chest, like before.

I want to tell you how I dreamed of you—

               How I pulled you from the reeds,
                   how I dreamed this for days
                         before the doctors called me in,
                    emergency c-section.
                   How I cupped you with one hand,
         touch filtered through holes in plexiglass.

Now you press your forehead
         against the glass of my Honda CRV,
       create as much space between us
     as if you could part the sea.
Leave me.

As I turn into our driveway,
your headphones roar.
I swallow my words; they sink,
layer my belly in stone.

But you do not know.
You open your door and go.
The sea crashes around me. I drown.

The Theory of Continental Drift
By Cassandra Mainiero

—for Alex

The theory of continental drift—

        another long-winded sermon on love:

connections

       fracture & shift

our control. In the world of *us,* imagine

you & *me*. I slink

       beneath you. You slide over

               me. Sometimes,

we slip,

       tremor & tremble,

reverberating   at magnitudes

          no seismometer

can scratch   no

magnetometer can track　　　no　　holy

summit can endure　　　　　　　　　　raining

　　　ash & burning laurels

in magma. What remains?

　　　Obsidian glass.

　　　　　　　　Fire.　　　　You see,　　　it's a mistake

to believe

　　　we won't　　drift.　We are not supernatural.　　　Nor

are we some sand-dollar Moon

　　　orbiting space like a counterweight,

preventing some cataclysmic

　　　wobble.　　Sex/love　　is radioactive

communion. It whirls

　　　　& warms water,

soundlessly, separately,

within *you*, within *me, &*

     us

the way   prayer

          clouds   between our laced
     fingers, a fallen
steeple.

Crossed Lines
By Michele Wolfe

Twenty-Something - 1988

The night in the motel on the Canada side of Niagara changes everything. It may have started before you ended up in bed with him, but you'll never know.

Three to the other bed, two to this one. You've been taking turns depending on the motel. An odd mix of friends and you the odd one out. Two good looking males, one definitely not your type. You're attracted to the one beside you on the sinking mattress, more than a bit. Two other females, best friends, make up your little band of travelers.

During the long days on the road trip from Denver, crammed in one car, you've discovered you don't have much in common with any of them. But you're good at pretending.

The girls, side by side, and not-your-type are fast asleep in the bed by the window. Even with the drapes closed, passing car lights create a shadow show on the interior wall. The one in your bed scoots over, wants to talk. In whispers he confesses he's into the other guy on the trip.

There goes your hope it was a mutual attraction. This midnight tete-a-tete creates a dilemma for the part of you that wants to belong. The part of you that's embarrassed you didn't catch the gay vibe going on. The part that always seems to acquiesce. You don't know why, but you lie. It's a small one. No big deal. That's cool, he's into you too, you reply. How do you know? he asks. He told me, you say. He smiles, turns over and joins them in la-la land.

The next day, the guys freeze you out. They certainly look cozier. Did they compare notes and find you out? You alternate between chatty and withdrawn, wondering what's going on. You try to engage them, recreate the camaraderie of the previous days, but they evade your questions.

It gets bleaker the closer you get to the Cape. The girls offer only the barest of civil discourse. You tumble inside yourself while pines tower over both sides of the road that leads through a town called Sandwich. Roadside lobster stands, clapboard houses, overturned boats are blurs as the car whizzes by. They talk, they joke, they laugh.

Once in Hyannis on the Cape, the girls in one adjoining room, the guys in the other, you discover it's easy to find jobs waiting tables and hostessing. Despite the mob of tanned good-looking twenty-somethings descending on this summer tourist town looking for work. You have experience.

You take two jobs, a lunch shift at a family-style restaurant and a dinner shift at an upscale dining place where you toss anchovies into the Caesar salads before serving and uncork bottles of wine at the table. You become more isolated than ever with these daily double shifts and little sleep. You have no energy to make new friends. A week, then two, become a blur.

One midnight as you're returning to a motel room you're beginning to hate, your feet take you through the parking lot to the lone pay phone you've never really noticed before. You pull out quarters from your apron full of tips. Dial home. They have been waiting for you to call. Check in. There's bad news. Your beloved Nana has died.

It's too much. The loneliness, the doubts about your choices, the fresh grief. The sky opens up with a drenching rain that becomes your tears. You sob a plea for a plane ticket home. But they don't have the money and neither do you. You are stuck.

When you finally go to the room, the four are waiting for you. They don't care that you are soaking wet. Or that your grandmother died. They had a pow-wow and want you gone. It's just not working out, they say.

Left alone while they party in the other room, you sit by the dripping window pane unable to sleep. Teeth chattering, you can't seem to get warm even after a hot shower and wrapping in a warm blanket.

Flashbacks of the past weeks thunder through your muddled brain. Did you sabotage the friendships with that lie? Or were they testing you and you failed? You haven't managed to figure them out but it seems they are taking the high road the low way. The biggest question smacks you in the face and wakes you out of the stupor you let be your default. Why did you stay so long?

First step. Looking through the want ads you find a room for rent. You call and arrange to meet. A sweet woman, the house a bit ramshackle, but close to one of the restaurants where you work. It'll do. It's less than what you've been paying and you'll be able to save. She'll even let you borrow a bicycle to get around town.

Second step. Find yourself. You took a detour because you weren't paying attention to the signs. Yes, you fucked up with the lie. But now is the time to make a plan of your own. No one else's. This is your life.

Third Step. Depend on no one but you.

Thirty-Something - 1998

You had no idea what you were getting yourself into when you agreed to this. One is enough, you said. He needs brothers and sisters to play with, he said. You compromised on only one more. It didn't take long. As soon as you stopped birth control, you were doing round two.

You manage to settle into a routine with preschool and park and mealtimes before you hand them over to their father when he returns from work. Then you leave to teach your night class. It's exhausting.

Ten years ago, you never could've imagined this life. Every day is a landscape of questions and doubts. From how long to breastfeed to whether you can afford a night out. Financially, you're barely getting by. You have a less than part-time job where you can get away for a few hours. Interact with adults. Be something other than mother. But if you worked more, would that even cover child care?

Now you sit in the car in the parking lot of 7-Eleven with a three-year-old in need of a nap in a booster seat behind you and a wailing six-month-old in the car seat next to him. The obvious stops you from undoing your seatbelt. You pulled in to get a gallon of milk. A spill this morning left little for the rest of the day. Should be easy. Grab your wallet, run in, get the milk and get out. Two minutes, tops. Wait. That is no longer an option.

You can't leave them in the car, although it's tempting. What could happen in two minutes? With your luck the cops who frequent here would pull up, see the two alone in the back seat and arrest you for child endangerment.

Neither will you unbuckle each of them, take one by the hand, the other in your arms, juggle car keys and wallet and go in. A three-year-old can't handle the temptation of the candy, cookies and chips that adorn the aisles. Plus, you'd lose hold of him in a second. You can see him grabbing for the least healthy item in the store and wanting it. Crying till he gets it.

You've had enough temper tantrums today without adding another. What were you thinking even stopping? Forget the milk.

The wailing stops. You turn to look. Older brother reaches over to pat his baby brother's sleeping brow. Sweet and fragile, the moment comes out of nowhere, leaving you astonished. You inhale deeply to breathe it in. Keep it close.

In a flash older brother has a hold of the baby's arm, puts it in his mouth and bites.

This time, not a worn-out wailing, but outright screaming commences. Before you can think, you smack your three-year-old on his cheek. He flinches, startled. He doesn't cry, but the hurt, the shock in his eyes is clear and mirrors your own.

His behavior is typical for a child his age. All the books say so. But you don't know how to get him to stop. Why did no one tell you how difficult motherhood would be? That they push all your buttons until you can't think straight. You vowed you would never hit your children. For any reason. But today you did.

Forty-Something – 2008

Naked from the waist up, you stand in the middle of a room, the faint outlines of a closet, dresser, vanity at the edges of sight. Hands drop a gauzy confection over your head that floats around you, settling on shoulders, over breasts. Covering you, of no more importance than that.

From a hanging mirror to your right, your reflection beckons. The features of your focus—eyes and lips. Wrinkles. Etched by years of smiles, frowns. You wish for a second to erase. But just like the scars you bear on hips, stomach, arms, legs, they mark the journey. You search the vanity drawer for one compact, an exact shade that, with sure brush strokes makes you complete.

Barefoot, you walk through a door, cross a street and enter the plaza. Alone but not alone. A presence behind you, always there, is you. Another faucet, dimension. Under a half-lidded gaze, you study paved walkways that stretch far in all directions. Market stalls in miniature lining the edges. Far flung sounds of sellers calling out their wares. Children running, playing, shrieking, laughing.

Your body knows the path, steps sure, the destination at the opposite end your focus. The growing darkness doesn't penetrate until walls appear. Not close, but close enough. Thousands of votive candles flicker, lending a smoky gloom that hangs in the air, coalescing out of reach.

A murmur of caution trails behind, but you brush it away. Walk straight through and you'll be fine. This is what you have been doing for some time now. Ignoring the edges. You eye your target, a haven just up ahead, and continue, pace casual.

All becomes silence, announcing true danger. From the depths of the now cavernous gray, red-robed men, staffs in hand, rise from wooden thrones in acknowledgment. Not of your approach, but of your notice. They have been waiting. This rising is a signal, a noiseless herald, as from all sides, out of the very walls, emerge young boys. White, cherub-faced and blond, garbed in ivory cassocks, angling their course to coincide with yours.

Fear explodes, a firecracker that propels your body into flight. You turn and run. A full, mad sprint back to the entrance. You are not an athlete, but a force propels you. Your feet no longer touch the ground. Only one vestment has caught up, running beside you. His young features exude confidence. He thinks he will get you. He'll get the prize.

You can see the end ahead, where the plaza meets the street. Intuition tells you once past plaza stones onto asphalt road you are untouchable. Vestment's gaze shifts to the force at your back. Doubt crosses his features, marring his beauty.

Rage is a boiling inferno, reaching, grasping. You pass the invisible line, reach the street and stop, your breathing labored, heart pounding. The plaza and its noise, inhabitants, fade away. You have escaped with your life.

You wake, twin feelings of fear and freedom fill your gut. Will you finally be brave enough now to name it? Or will the fear win and keep you silent?

The blood trickles from your hand down, dripping off the elbow. Your arm hangs in the air, suspended. Caught. You register the red on the white tile floor in a brief moment of surprise. It didn't even hurt. Just a tug as the stainless steel, long-shank barbed fishhook slipped into flesh.

Why did you ever agree to use twelve of these dangling by delicate chains from the curtain rod at the ceiling to hang the shower curtain? You are usually more careful when you unhook it to put it in the wash. But you were distracted and look where it landed you.

Your cell sits on the counter. You grab it with your left hand, now slippery with blood and sweat. You dial your husband. He's at a meeting. Turned off his phone. Next your neighbor. It rings and rings.

Paper towel up your hand and your arm smears the blood, but at least it's not dripping anymore. You actually consider just yanking the damn thing out but you're not sure it will work considering how deep it is buried right where your pinky meets your palm.

Breath is shallow. Think. Sweat breaks out across your brow. Think.

You dial 9-1-1. Talk it through with the nice woman on the other end. You glance up to the rod at the ceiling, the sterling silver chains that drop and end with the hooks that hold the curtain. You see your way out. So easy. How did it not occur to you before? No need to send the paramedics. Standing on top of the toilet, left hand unsteady, it takes a couple of tries before you're able to unhook the chain attached to the rod. Right hand trembles as it's released. You step down and gently wrap a towel around hand, hook and chain.

Your brain goes off panic mode and becomes laser-focused. Find keys and purse. Lock up house. Walk to car. Open door. Start engine. Drive. Stop at lights. Drive. Park. Walk into ER. Show nurse.

The other people in the waiting room can't help but stare when you unfold the towel. Then look away, embarrassed. You try to get through to your husband again. This time he answers. Minutes stretch. Your morning replays over and over until he arrives. Tears come as he walks through the door. You got this far but now you are not alone with whatever this is.

It is not about a fish hook. Or your propensity for accidents. It is about the long-distance phone conversation yesterday with your father.

The doc and nurse ask, so you tell the tale of how the fish hook ended up in your finger. To your ears it sounds like a bizarre but minor accident. Still, random-white-coat and bright-color-scrubbed people keep stopping by to take a look.

To ease the long wait, your husband jokes. Takes pictures. Sends them to family. You smile through the throbbing pain. Your finger has become the state of your heart. Stabbed, bleeding, hurt. You don't know exactly when the just-yesterday conversation that feels like forever-ago went so awry, but once politics was brought up, you should've shut it down.

After all these years, you are still so confounded by the disconnect between what your father says is his faith and his political beliefs. It's a mystery for which you want an answer, but are finally realizing you'll never get.

After X-rays and back and forth between docs, they numb your finger, slice a bit and pull the fish hook out. Plop it in a small plastic tub to take home as a souvenir. After a few stitches and pain meds you are released.

Trying to make a point, using a question you think will illustrate best the disconnect of his beliefs, the very way he raised you, you bring up the current events of the day. A woman testifying before the government, in front of the world, the sexual misconduct of a white male of privilege. What if that woman was I? you ask. What if I had been raped in college? What if he assaulted me and it was me up there testifying? Wouldn't you believe me?

You leave the ER, trying to remember where you parked the car. Are you sure you are okay to drive? your partner asks. You nod, your head and heart clear. Your hand now sporting a white gauze mitt, you drive yourself home. He follows.

The shocking answer that shut you down, that you buried in your sleep last night and distracted you until the blood dripped down your arm.

She is lying, your father said.

You wrap up your heart until the bleeding stops, the gauze no longer red, but white.

Months later, an almost imperceptible scar graces the inside of your small finger. The scar on your heart is another matter. You have not spoken to him since that day. Will you ever again?

Contributors:

Cover Artist:

Gregg Chadwick has exhibited his artworks in galleries and museums both nationally and internationally. He earned a Bachelor's Degree at UCLA and a Master's Degree at NYU, both in Fine Art. He has had notable solo exhibitions at the Manifesta Maastricht Gallery (Maastricht, The Netherlands), Space AD 2000 (Tokyo, Japan), the Lisa Coscino Gallery (Pacific Grove, CA), the Julie Nester Gallery (Park City, Utah), the Sandra Lee Gallery (San Francisco), and Audis Husar Fine Arts (Los Angeles) among others. He has participated in over one hundred group exhibitions including the L Ross Gallery (Memphis, Tennessee), the Andrea Schwartz Gallery (San Francisco), the LOOK Gallery (Los Angeles), the di Rosa Preserve Gallery (Napa), and the Arts Club of Washington (Washington DC). Chadwick's artwork has been featured at Saatchi Art's The Other Art Fair in Los Angeles, Dallas, and Chicago, Aqua Art Miami, artMRKT San Francisco, the Palm Springs Fine Art Fair, and the LA Art Show. Chadwick's art is notably included in the collections of the Adobe Corporation, the Gilpin Museum, the Central City Opera, the Graciela Hotel Burbank, the Harbor Court Hotel, the Kimpton, Nordstrom, the W Hotel Hollywood, the UCLA School of Nursing, and Winona State University. Chadwick is frequently invited to lecture on the arts; twice a year he delivers a key lecture on art and social justice at UCLA in an interdisciplinary form with the UCLA School of Nursing, and has spoken at Monterey Peninsula College, the Esalen Institute, and at the World Views forum in Amsterdam, The Netherlands. In Winter 2020, Chadwick was a working artist in residence at the Center Theatre Group in Los Angeles leading students at Culver City High School in an exploration of Dael Orlandersmith's "Until the Flood." Chadwick is the proud father of his transgender daughter Cassiel Chadwick.

About Carpe Librum (Maastricht): Books are magic. They hold time between their bindings like a memory vault. Libraries and bookstores are reliquaries of stories. Wandering the aisles of a bookstore, I often lose track of time as I open the cover of a new book and enter into the author's world. My oil on linen painting "Carpe Librum (Maastricht)" was created as an homage to dreamlike days spent in bookshops across the globe. In the past few years, a magnificent bookstore in Maastricht, The Netherlands—Boekhandel Dominicanen—has inspired a group of my oil paintings and works on paper. Housed in a former church, gothic windows and fading frescoes provide memories of the past. Modern lighting and the hiss of the espresso machine in the bookstore's café keep us tethered to the present. Carpe Librum—seize the book.

"Carpe Librum (Maastricht)", 48"x36", oil on Belgian linen, 2021 Collection of Dani Durkin and Dave Lowther, Brentwood, California

Matthew Birch grew up in London and now studies Law at Keele University. He has come Highly Commended in the 2016 Foyle's Young Poet of the Year Award, the 2018 University of Lincoln Armistice 100 competition and was shortlisted for the 2019 Erbacce poetry prize.

Mark Blackford, a native of New York's once famed Borscht Belt, has had work recently appear in *High Shelf Press, Glassworks*, and *Cathexis Northwest Press*, with new work forthcoming in *Oyez Review*. He was a 2020 Pushcart nominee and, once, read his poetry to open for Arlo Guthrie (unpaid). He resides in Bushkill, PA with his family, and is presently the Chapbook Editor for *The Chestnut Review*.

Barbara Daniels' *Talk to the Lioness* was published by Casa de Cinco Hermanas Press. Her poetry has appeared in *Permafrost, Westchester Review, Philadelphia Stories, Coachella Review*, and many other journals. She has received four fellowships from the New Jersey State Council on the Arts.

Cat Dixon (she/her) is a Pushcart Prize and Best of the Net nominee. She is the author of *Eva* and *Too Heavy to Carry* (Stephen F. Austin University Press, 2016, 2014) and the chapbook, *Table for*

Two (Poet's Haven, 2019). Recent work published in *Sledgehammer Lit* and *Whale Road Review*. She is a poetry editor at *The Good Life Review*.

Abbie Doll is an eclectic mess of a person who loves exploring the beautiful intricacies of the written word. She resides in Columbus, OH and received her MFA from Lindenwood University; her work has been featured in *Cathexis Northwest Press, The Rush, OPEN: Journal of Arts & Letters (O:JA&L)*, among others. Follow her @AbbieDollWrites.

Tyra Douyon is a writer, editor, and educator. She earned her B.A. in English Education and is pursuing her M.A. in Professional Writing from Kennesaw State University. She is the founder of Write House Books, a freelance editing company, and is a staff Writer/Editor for Gallopade International and serves as Co-Editorial Director for *The Headlight Review*. She writes poetry and fiction that highlight the effects of mental health and the intersection of Afro-Caribbean and American identity. Her poetry has appeared in *Josephine Quarterly, Muse, Paper Dragon, Storm Cellar, Aunt Chloe, Black Fox*, and others. She was accepted into the 2022 cohort of the Tin House Writer's Workshop and is currently writing her first poetry collection. You can find her filling her shopping cart with too many flowers and visiting national parks with her dog, Mya. Website: tyradouyon.com

Melissa Ridley Elmes is a Virginia native currently living in Missouri in an apartment that delightfully approximates a hobbit hole. Her poetry and fiction have appeared in *Star*Line, Eye to the Telescope, In Parentheses, Gyroscope Review, Thimble Magazine,* and various other print and web venues, and her first collection of poems, *Arthurian Things*, was published by Dark Myth Publications in 2020. Follow her on Twitter and Instagram @MRidleyElmes.

Jacqueline Garlitos recently moved from New Jersey to Idaho in order to have more time to write. After receiving her MFA in 2004, she has been a finalist/semifinalist for several national awards.

Melissa Grunow is the author of *I Don't Below Here: Essays* (New Meridian Arts Press, 2018), finalist in the 2019 Independent Author Network Book of the Year Award and 2019 Best Indie Book from Shelf Unbound, and *Realizing River City: A Memoir* (Tumbleweed Books, 2016) which won the 2018 Book Excellence Award in Memoir, the 2017 Silver Medal in Nonfiction-Memoir from Readers' Favorite International Book Contest, and Second Place-Nonfiction in the 2016 Independent Author Network Book of the Year Awards. Her work has appeared in *Brevity, River Teeth, The Nervous Breakdown, Two Hawks Quarterly, New Plains Review, Blue Lyra Review*, and many others. Her essays have been nominated for a Pushcart Prize and Best of the Net, as well as listed in the Best American Essays notables 2016, 2018, 2019, and 2020. She is an associate professor of English at Illinois Central College.

Keith LaFountaine is a writer from Vermont and a member of the Horror Writers Association. His short fiction has appeared in *Dread Stone Press, Literally Stories*, and *Five on the Fifth*. Other work, including forthcoming stories, can be found on his website, www.keithlafountaine.com.

Gary Lark's most recent collections are *Easter Creek, Main Street Rag, Daybreak on the Water, Flowstone Press* and *Ordinary Gravity*, Airlie Press. His work has appeared in *Beloit Poetry Journal, Catamaran, Rattle, Sky Island* and others.

Cassandra Mainiero's poetry has been published in *Sigma Tau Delta Journal, Mind Murals, The New Jersey Journal of Poets, West Branch Wired*, and more. She holds a bachelor's in English from Lycoming College and an MFA in Writing from Vermont College of Fine Arts. Currently, she is working to complete her first chapbook.

Christopher Milligan earned a BA from Marquette University with majors in English and American History. In 2015, his manuscript, *Riding the Pine*, was short-listed in the William Faulkner-James Jones creative writing competition novel-in-progress category. Nature, the dynamics of small towns, and baseball are his inspiration. Christopher lives in Arizona with his wife, Terri, and their dogs, Ranger and Scout. He is a steward at the McDowell Sonoran Conservancy. He is editing his manuscript, *Riding the Pine*, as well as a collection of short stories entitled *After*.

Florence Murry is the author of *Last Run Before Sunset* forthcoming in 2023. Her poems have appeared in *Slipstream Press, Stoneboat Literary Magazine, Off the Coast, Bluestem Magazine, Southern California Review, Rockhurst Review, Hole In The Head Review* and others. Her poem "Exhumed" received an Honorable Mention in *Cultural Weekly*, Annual Jack Grapes Contest, 2015. Florence is a member of Jack Grapes' L.A. Poets and Writers Collective. She, her husband, and two cats live in a Mid-Century Modern home in Southern California.

Chelsie Blair Nunn (she/they) is an LGBTQIA+ artist and educator working in Knoxville, TN. They have collaboratively mentored graduate students entering the visual art education field from the University of Tennessee Knoxville for the past seven years. Their painting and writing primarily investigates the sublime nature of contradictory thoughts, images, beliefs, and experiences as they congregate in one's mental landscape.

Sophia Ordaz is a Chicana writer based in Arkansas. You can reliably find her in a mosh pit, on her longboard, or in bed reading a book. She occasionally tweets at @krzykittensmile and rants and raves about music at @auralwhiplash.

Michelle Ott is an emerging poet from the Mid-Atlantic. She is an MFA student at American University earning her degree in Creative Writing, and also serves as the Community Outreach Coordinator for the university's literary magazine, *FOLIO*. Her poetry has previously been published in Volume 14 of the Northern Virginia Writers' Project's anthology *Falling for the Story*, and will be featured in the upcoming 2022 DC Pride Poem a Day project. She currently lives in Washington, D.C., and regularly travels across the Potomac to see her childhood dog.

Christina E. Petrides teaches English on Jeju Island, South Korea. Her first poetry collection, *On Unfirm Terrain*, is forthcoming from Kelsay Books. Christina's website is: www.christinaepetrides.com.

Kate Porch (she/her/hers) was born and raised in South Florida as one in a loving family of seven. She is an emerging writer, and holds a BA in creative writing from the University of Central Florida. Kate's most recent adventure has been uprooting her comfortable Floridian life to move to Thailand, where she is now living life to the fullest and holds a full-time job as a primary school teacher. In her free time, she loves to explore the world around her, learn new languages, and curl up on the couch with a good book and a cup of tea. Follow her on Twitter: @misskateleigh.

Gary Reddin grew up among the cicada songs and tornado sirens of Southwest Oklahoma. His writing was born in this dissonance. He refuses to experience any emotion on a small scale, preferring instead to turn everything into a grand ordeal.

Andréa Rivard earned her MFA in Fiction at the University of Massachusetts, Boston in 2022. Her background is in English Education, and she still tutors English online. She's currently working on her first novel for young adults. She lives with her husband and cats in central Mass. Her fiction has been published or is upcoming in *The Gateway Review, Youth Imagination Magazine,* and elsewhere.

Laura Rockhold is a poet and visual artist living in Minnesota. She is the inventor of the golden root poetic form, and is working on her first collection of poetry and a multidisciplinary art exhibition that explores the interconnectedness of environmental and social issues and healing. Her work appears or is forthcoming in *Variety Pack, Quail Bell Magazine, swifts & slows, Black Fox Literary Magazine* and *The Hopper.* She holds a B.S. in child psychology from the University of Minnesota. Her website is www.laurarockhold.com.

Victoria Elizabeth Ruwi is the author of *Eye Whispers*, a book of poetry. She earned an MFA in Creative Writing from San Diego State University. Her writing has been published in journals and anthologies all over the states, most recently the *North Dakota Review, Pegasus,* and *Thin Air.* She feeds stray cats.

Nic Sattavara is a queer writer from Michigan. They earned their MFA from the University of Alabama. Their work has appeared in *temenos, Cimarron Review,* and *Red Ogre Review.*

Kat Stubing was born into the sticky heat of summer and has been searching for the right words ever since. Her poems have been published in *Beyond Words, Hare's Paw,* and *The Closed Eye Open.* Kat lives, works, and dreams in New York City. Find Kat at: katjoys.squarespace.com.

Theresa Sylvester is a Zambian writer based in Western Australia. She has short stories published in *Black Warrior Review, Midnight and Indigo,* and in Australia's Rockingham Writers Centre 2019 anthology.

Stephanie Trenchard, a visual artist working primarily in hot glass out of her Wisconsin studio, creates works that reference the experience of women artists throughout history. In contrast to her once-molten-glass sculptures, which can be found in museums and collections, writing and publishing poetry is one of her cooler passions. Her poetry can be found in *The Dillydoun Review* and *Writers.com.*

Nikki Ummel is a queer writer, editor, and educator in New Orleans. Nikki has been published or is forthcoming in *Painted Bride Quarterly, The Adroit Journal, The Georgia Review,* and more. She has been nominated for a Pushcart Prize, Best New Poets, and twice awarded an Academy of American Poets Award. She is the 2022 winner of the Leslie McGrath Poetry Prize. Her chapbook, *Hush*, is forthcoming from Belle Point Press (2022). You can find her on the web at www.nikkiummel.com.

Loren Walker is a twice-nominated Pushcart Prize nominee and a finalist in the Beulah Rose Poetry Contest. Her poems have appeared in *Hive Avenue Literary Journal, QU Journal, the West Texas Literary Review, Perch Magazine,* and *Sugared Water*, among other publications. She has self-published two chapbooks: *dislocation* and *strong water*; her micro-chapbook *neverheart* was published by Dancing Girl Press in 2021. Loren is also the author of award-winning fantasy and science-fiction novels, a linocut printmaker, and embroidery artist; she lives in Providence, Rhode Island.

Patheresa Wells is a queer poet, writer, and storyteller. Born to a Black mother and Persian father in the Midwest, she has called the Pacific Northwest home for twenty-plus years. Her poetry is inspired by her experiences with poverty, loneliness, and what it means to be a writer, though she finds inspiration everywhere. In her spare time, she enjoys gardening, traveling, and feeding crows.

Shamon Williams earned a BS in psychology and a BA in English at the University of Central Florida. When she isn't working, writing, or taking yet another catnap, she voice acts. Shamon's work can be found in *Hive Avenue Literary Journal, Bluffton University Literary Journal, Dreamers Creative Writing and Brooklyn Poets* and more.

Michele Wolfe is a fiction writer, author of one novel, *The Three Graces*, a memoir piece in *LA Affairs* of *The LA Times*, and two short stories published in *Lunch Ticket* and *Five on the Fifth*. She lives in a 1922 bungalow in Echo Park in Los Angeles with her husband, finding inspiration in bustling city life and walks in the hills of Elysian Park. When not writing, she can be found at museums, libraries and bookstores, wine tasting, and gardening. You can follow her on Instagram @authormichelewolfe.

Kristin Wong is a writer and journalist whose work has appeared in *The New York Times, The Atlantic, Catapult*, and *ELLE* among other publications.

*We love seeing photos of our issues online, as well as people reading Black Fox! Please tag us in your photos and videos so we can share also!

Thank you for reading! Stay in touch:

www.blackfoxlitmag.com
Website

www.facebook.com/blackfoxlit
Facebook

@blackfoxlit
Twitter & Instagram

www.blackfoxlitmag.com/contact/
Newsletter

Check out some of our previous issues:

Resources for Writers from BFLM Editor Racquel Henry's Writer's Atelier:

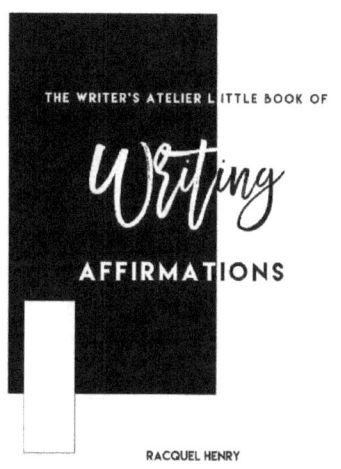

The Writer's Atelier Little Book of Writing Affirmations

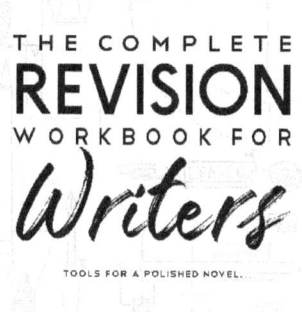

The Complete Revision Workbook for Writers

www.ingramcontent.com/pod-product-compliance
Lightning Source LLC
Chambersburg PA
CBHW060945180626
46817CB00004B/1715